MAGIC WILD

Dragon's Gift: The Seeker Book 4

Linsey Hall

DEDICATION

To the Tiki Bar Masterminds. You guys are the
best.

CHAPTER ONE

Rain pattered on the dark cobblestones, and the smell of black magic permeated the alley. It had a distinctly rotten scent I knew I wouldn't be able to shake for hours.

And it didn't help that we were hidden behind a dumpster.

All in all, not my favorite way to spend an evening.

A rustling sounded from the other end of the lane, and I pressed myself against the wall, glancing at my friend Claire. Her dark hair and dark leather helped her blend into Darklane, the part of the city that housed Magic Bend's black magic users. The whole place was dark as coal, coated in residue from the shady spells that were common here.

"Think that's him?" I whispered.

"Good chance." She stood stock-still, her sword gripped comfortably in her hand, ever ready. The consummate mercenary.

Her most recent job from the Order of the Magica was to hunt down a Telenec demon. He'd eaten the mayor and her husband. They'd both actually been real jerks, trying to enforce racist policies, but still…

You shouldn't eat people.

So, the Telenec demon was going down.

Claire had let me come along because I wanted to steal the Telenec demon's powers. Telekinesis would be a handy skill to have, and I was committed to building my arsenal if I was going to win whatever battle was coming my way, brought by the Shadows from my past. Worry had been dogging me for the last week, a demon on my back that I couldn't shake. I didn't know what I was going to be up against, but fear that I couldn't handle it was ever present.

We'd tracked the Telenec demon through information from his colleagues and learned that he'd be visiting a secret gambling den tonight.

So we were hanging out behind a dumpster, waiting for our prey to amble past. Lurking like two giant, smelly spiders.

Finally, footsteps thudded down the alley. I exchanged a disgusted glance with Claire. We both valued sneakiness. This guy lacked it.

From my vantage point behind the dumpster, I wouldn't be able to see who it was till he passed by, so I reached out with my magic, feeling for his.

At first, all I got was the very subtle scent of Claire's power. It smelled like smoke and warmed my skin. Claire was part Fire Mage and part Hearth Witch, but the Fire Mage was stronger. I pushed harder, straining my senses.

I was hit by the feeling of wind against my skin, though the night was calm.

Definitely the Telenec demon, then. That was definitely a signature that would accompany the ability to move things with your mind.

A moment later, he walked past the dumpster. I craned my neck, catching sight of his back as he strolled down the alley. He was tall, at least six and a half feet, and could have almost passed for human in his dark jeans and leather jacket. His horns were hidden by a mass of dark hair, but I knew they were small and black from the image I'd seen in one of my books.

He ducked into a doorway about twenty feet down the alley.

"Let's move," I said.

"On it."

We hurried out from behind the dumpster, racing down the alley on silent feet.

"Knock on wood," I muttered as we sidled up to the door.

Claire grinned at my superstition, then knocked on her head. I did the same, hoping the place wasn't too crowded.

We didn't know what to expect in the gambling den. Recon had been impossible because it was members only, and we weren't welcome.

It'd have been better to nab him out in the alley, but part of the job was catching his partner, who was supposed to meet him here. Claire would take one, I would take the other, and we'd hope we didn't get caught in something nasty.

Claire sheathed her sword, but she'd have her fire ready. My blade was stored in the ether, but I probably wouldn't need it. Not as long as I had my gift over ice.

We shared a last glance, then I pushed open the door and strolled inside.

Smoke choked me almost immediately. Not just cigarette smoke—though there were plenty of cigarettes—but some kind of heavy black smoke that hung in the air. For atmosphere?

Not a fan.

The place was small but crowded, little tables set up here and there with species of all sorts huddled around, each holding a handful of Enchanta Cards. The game was popular here in Darklane, though I didn't know the rules. Thick mugs of dark beer were cluttered on tables, and the little bar at the back was manned by a supernatural who glowed faintly green.

Heads turned toward us, confusion and boredom on various faces.

I ignored them, taking in the room as I headed to the bar. We didn't blend in here, but there was no reason to stand stock-still, staring like dopes. And the Telenec demon didn't know Claire had been hired to find him, so that gave us an element of surprise.

I stopped at the bar.

"Are you meeting a member here?" The bartender's voice was sibilant, his eyes a brilliant green. Snake shifter, maybe?

"Yeah," I said. "My friend Mordaca invited us."

She was a member here. It had cost a pretty penny to get her to let us use her name, but it satisfied the bartender, who nodded. "What'll it be?"

I doubted they served wine here, even my cheap boxed stuff, so I pointed to the single tap behind the bar. "Beer."

"Same for me," Claire said.

He nodded and turned, grabbing two glasses and pulling the beer tap.

"I'll keep an eye out." I turned, leaning back against the bar and gazing around the room, trying to look bored.

It was hard, though. The variety of species was huge—and most were the violent sort. Demons, monsters, possibly one vampire. I shuddered. There were so many people crowded into the little space, sitting or standing or making out in corners, that it was hard to spot my target.

Claire thanked the bartender and paid, then turned and handed me a beer. She raised her drink to her mouth. "Find him?"

"No, not—"

My gaze caught on a man in the corner. His dark hair and pale skin were semi-obscured by the smoke. He had his elbows propped on a table and was having an intense conversation with another demon. My hand faltered, my beer stopping just short of my lips.

"Holy fates," I breathed.

He was somewhat tall and looked almost exactly like my boyfriend. My heart raced, and the hair on my arms stood on end.

Caden, Roarke's brother. Who Roarke was currently hunting for. At this very minute.

He'd fallen right into my lap.

"Change of plans." I set my beer on the bar. "I have to catch that guy."

"What about the demon?" Claire tilted her chin toward our target, who was on the other side of the room, now meeting with his buddy, a stocky demon whose skin looked like old shoe leather.

"Shit." I was Claire's only backup. To bring both in, she'd need a hand. Torn, I glanced back to Roarke's brother.

He was turning toward me, as if he sensed my gaze. When his eyes met mine, they widened.

My heart jumped. Before I could step forward, he leaped to his feet. The air around him shimmered briefly before his form turned into black mist. The ephemeral dust swirled in the air and disappeared, shooting out the door.

What the hell? Frustration welled within me, beating its fists against my ribs.

The shock threw the bar into commotion. People surged to their feet, chairs toppling as beer spilled. It spooked the demon we were after, and he bolted.

"I'll take him. Get the other!" I said. Caden was gone, but I still had a chance with the demon.

We split up as my target pushed through the room, shoving people out of his way. I rushed toward him, unable to get a clear shot to throw an icicle. When he was right across from me, his gaze darted to mine, catching me headed straight for him.

Confusion flashed in his dark eyes right before he waved a hand toward me, flicking his wrist in a weird movement.

A table hurtled through the air, flying toward my head. I ducked just in time, but the demon sent a chair next.

It slammed into my side. I stumbled.

Damned telekinesis.

By the time I righted myself, he was at the back door. He disappeared through it. I shoved past the crowd, having to deck a guy who stood belligerently in my way. His nose crunched beneath my fist, and he toppled backward.

I leaped over him and raced outside.

The alley was empty—not even a dumpster in sight, thank magic. The walls loomed high on either side, but the moon peeked through, reflecting on the damp streets. The demon sped down the alley, too far away for me to ever catch on foot.

I called upon my magic, letting the chill of ice flow though me. When the power had filled me, I released it, sending a semi-frozen stream of slush toward him. It splashed against his feet, freezing instantly. It didn't freeze him to the ground, but he tripped and stumbled, crashing onto his front.

I sprinted toward him, lungs burning. As I neared, he scrambled upright, and I shot an icicle at his back. It pierced his chest, and he stumbled forward, landing in a pile.

Panting, I jumped on him, flipping him over. The icicle broke beneath him. Blood pooled on the cobblestones. He snarled at me, but the sound was weak. He had fangs, horrible yellow ones, and I gagged at the thought of them tearing into the mayor's flesh.

"Why'd you eat them?" I couldn't help but ask. It was just so *gross*.

"Tasty." He gurgled, blood dripping from the corner of his mouth.

Ew. "Well, you should have stuck to donuts."

He coughed, his chest jerking around the ice I'd send into him. As he gasped his last breath, I called on my Phantom form. My skin chilled, and my body turned the familiar transparent blue.

His soul was ephemeral and felt like mist against my fingertips. It was a pale white ghost of a thing, and I pulled it from his body. It came easily, absorbing into me. The whole process calmed some of the worry that had been constantly niggling in my chest. Just this act of stealing his power felt like I was taking charge of my fate. For the first time in a week, I felt in control.

I let his power sink into me, enjoying it. The breeze that was his signature rushed over me again, ruffling my hair.

It was eerie, but I'd get used to it.

I'd have to. This power was mine, now. Forever.

Finished, I hopped up. My knees were cold where blood had soaked through my jeans. "Ugh."

Footsteps sounded behind me. I whirled.

Claire sauntered down the alley, sword dangling at her side. "I see you finished."

"Yep. All done."

"Get his power?"

I nodded. It had felt *good*. "I'll test it out later."

I was worried about side effects. How could I not be, after everything that had happened? But I was going to need more powers if I wanted to survive whatever was coming for me. Since I couldn't outrun my past, I needed to fight it.

We'd met the Shadows only a week ago when rescuing Draka. The ghosts from my past had been hunting me and had nearly succeeded in catching me. The learning that I was their "Queen" and meant to play a role in a deadly plot had been a real mind-screw. Since I didn't want to be their creepy queen, I'd need magic to fight whatever they planned for me.

"Just let me know when you practice. I don't want to get hit by wayward objects." Claire pulled her cell phone out of her pocket and snapped pictures of the demon's body. She then knelt and fished around under his shirt collar. When she came up with a silver charm on a leather strap, she yanked it off him and stood. "Evidence for the Order."

"Of course." Normally, the demon's body would disappear back to his Underworld, so mercenaries were required to provide other evidence that they'd completed their work. But since I'd stolen the demon's soul, his body wouldn't disappear as normal. "You sure you don't mind burning him?"

"Not at all." She glanced around the alley. When she was satisfied that no one was around, she held out her hands and shot a jet of flame at the demon.

Her magic smelled strong and bright, like a campfire. But soon, the scent of burning demon flesh made me gag.

"Yeah, better hold your breath." She fed the blaze more flame. It was immensely hot, stronger than any fire I'd ever seen. Within twenty seconds, the demon's body was entirely gone. The only evidence was a burn scar on the cobblestones.

"Thanks, Claire." If only all my messes could be cleaned up so easily.

When we arrived at P & P after disposing of the Telenec demon's body, the doors were locked. It was just after midnight, closing time, and Connor was inside sweeping the floor. Claire dug her keys out of her pocket and unlocked the glass door.

I followed her into the warmly lit space that still smelled of baked goods and coffee. Cass and Nix sat in our favorite squishy chairs in the corner, polishing off their drinks. Chill music played over the speakers, something I'd never heard before—which wasn't unusual, considering Connor's eclectic taste in music— but I liked it.

"Hey!" Cass called.

"You look like you need a drink," Nix said.

"Do I ever." And food. My stomach grumbled loudly.

Connor looked up from his work, his dark hair flopped over his forehead. "Success?"

"Yep!" For the first time, I called upon my new magic, letting it flow through me like a soft breeze. It was the weirdest feeling. I didn't really know where to start with telekinesis, so I did what I always did with new magic. I envisioned what I wanted.

It didn't work.

Instead of a chair shifting so that Connor could sweep under it, it flipped to the floor with a crash.

I grimaced. "Looks like I could use some practice."

Claire patted my shoulder. "You'll get there."

Connor righted the chair. "In the meantime, stay away from the glassware."

I smiled.

"Help yourself." He gestured to the counter where the day's leftovers were laid out on plates.

I spied a single slice of quiche and grinned. "Thanks!"

Claire and I wove though the tables and set upon the food like wolves. I picked up the quiche and took a bite—no fork for this heathen, thanks—and Claire bit into a scone.

"I never thought we'd get out of that alley," she muttered around a mouthful.

I swallowed the savory mushroom quiche. "No kidding. Had to be hours."

"It was. Three."

I polished off the last of the quiche and slipped behind the bar, filling a coffee mug halfway full from the boxed merlot that they kept on hand for me.

"Pour me one of those, will you?" Claire asked.

"Anytime." I filled her mug and passed it over.

"Thanks."

We crossed the coffee shop and took our seats next to Cass and Nix. The plush leather chair enveloped me like a hug.

"Successful job, then?" Nix asked.

"Yep." I sipped my wine. "Now I just need to learn to use the telekinesis."

"It's a good skill," Cass said. "It'll come in handy."

"That's my hope."

"The best you can do is stock up on powers, learn to use them, and stay alert," Nix said. "We'll figure this out."

"Weird thing, though," I said. "I swore I saw—"

Someone knocked on the glass door to P & P. I spun to see who would come at this late hour.

Roarke and Aidan stood on the other side of the glass, both wearing dark jackets and blending into the night. They'd been on the hunt for Roarke's brother, visiting a contact that Aidan had in Darklane. I'd tried to help find Caden using my dragon sense but hadn't been able to get a lead on him. He likely wore a powerful concealment charm, which he'd need, considering he was on the run from the Order after escaping their prison.

"I got it." Claire hopped up and let them in.

They stepped into the shop, both towering over Claire, who wasn't a short woman.

"Speak of the devil," I said.

"Not literally." Roarke grinned. "Just the Warden."

They approached. Though Aidan was technically a good-looking guy by all accounts, I only had eyes for Roarke. My gaze was glued to his tall, muscular form. He looked like he wrangled demons for a living, which he did. His dark hair and eyes gleamed under the warm lights of the coffee shop. A grin curled his full lips as his eyes met mine.

"Hey." His voice was rough, lowered.

I shivered. "Hey."

He leaned down and pressed a kiss to my lips. Warmth flowed through me at the brief touch. I gripped his strong bicep and held him to me a moment longer, then pulled back.

"Successful trip?" He took a seat near me.

"Yeah. More than I expected." I glanced around at everyone. Aidan had taken a seat next to Cass. "I saw your brother."

Roarke's brows shot high. "Did you, now?"

"Yeah. He was at the gambling den where we caught the Telenec demon. I was going to try to nab him, but as soon as he saw me, he turned to black mist and disappeared."

Roarke frowned. "That's a new talent."

"It is?"

Roarke nodded. "Last I knew, he was half demon like me. How he got a new power, I have no idea. He's not part FireSoul or anything like that."

We were one of the very few species who could steal powers. In fact, until I'd learned that I could use my Phantom form to steal demon powers, I hadn't even known there was another species that could steal powers.

"I wonder how he got it, then?" I asked.

"I don't know, but I assume that's how he got out of prison," Roarke said.

"Makes sense," Aidan said. "There's pretty much no way to escape the Order prison unless you have powerful, dark magic."

"Or good friends," Cass added.

I grinned. We'd helped her and Emile escape the Order prison a few months ago. It hadn't been easy, but we'd managed.

"Either way, that's good information," Roarke said. "Aidan and I were able to track down Caden's supposed home base. If we're going to go after him, we need to know what he can use against us."

"So you found him, then?" I asked.

Aidan nodded. "My friend had heard of a half demon living in Florida who met Caden's description."

"Florida?" Nix asked. "You mean, land of retirees and gators."

"The very one," Roarke said. "Apparently, he's got a little place in the Everglades. Far off the beaten path."

I nodded. "All right. He's trying to lie low. Can't blame him."

"But if he's sided with the Shadows, wouldn't he stick close to them?" Cass asked. "Their headquarters are in Germany, right?"

"Not sure," Roarke said. "We didn't learn anything other than his potential location."

"Then we'll go after him. See what he knows about the Shadows." Worry tugged at me as I said the name. But almost as soon as the words left my lips, I slapped a hand over my mouth. "Shit, I'm sorry. This is about you and your brother. Not everything is about me."

I'd been so obsessed with everything that I'd learned about my past lately that I'd forgotten Roarke hadn't seen his brother in years. Ever since he'd tried to save him from the bad stuff he'd gotten into. And failed.

Roarke squeezed my hand. "Don't worry about it. This can be about both. As much as I'd love to find my brother and for everything to be great, it's not going to happen. He's committed the blackest magic. Killed people. I've come to terms with it. At this point, it's all about figuring out what's coming."

I tightened my grip on his, my heart clenching at the sadness on his face. He'd really loved his brother. Just because Caden had done some terrible things didn't mean that Roarke could forget loving him.

"So, we'll go find him." I nodded decisively. "And bring something to neutralize his ability to escape using his mist." I was glad I'd seen him at the gambling den, or we'd have blown it when we finally found him.

"My thoughts exactly," Roarke said.

"I think I can help you with that." Connor approached, broom propped over his shoulder. "A freezing charm should keep him from running for it."

"And my dampening charm—the bracelet that neutralizes powers," Cass said. I'd helped her steal the bracelet from a pyramid once. She'd worn it for a while to help control her crazy powers. "You can have that. If you freeze him and then slap the bracelet on him, he shouldn't be able to get away when he wakes up."

"Thanks, guys."

"You'll just need to make sure he doesn't pull the bracelet off," Cass said.

"I'll take care of it." Good thing I'd stolen the metal magic last week. It looked like I'd have to use it in the swamp. Along with who knew what else.

CHAPTER TWO

After a long shower to scrub off the demon blood and a good night's sleep, I set about selecting my battle garb.

Not only was Caden important to Roarke, he might have answers for me. Answers that I desperately wanted. The *not knowing* was starting to eat at me, wearing me down.

That meant pulling out the big guns. I selected a lucky pendant and two lucky bracelets—a matching set of Arctic silver crafted by the ice people of the north—along with a lucky T-shirt that had been bought at Target on a rare trip to a human city. Some things were made to be lucky—like the silver jewelry—and other things just turned out to be that way. The shirt had served me well on several demon-hunting expeditions last year and had been upgraded to a lucky item. I then chose my oldest—and most trusted—leather pants and jacket.

Properly outfitted, with my sword stored in the ether and the bracelet Cass had given me in my jacket pocket, I hurried down the stairs and out into the cool morning air. It was nearly the holidays now, and Oregon was letting us know it'd be a chilly one.

"Hey!" I waved at Roarke, who waited for me outside of P & P. Because he'd spent so much time lately helping me with my problems and hunting his brother, he'd had to head back to the Underworld last night to deal with some issues.

"Hey." He grinned at me and approached, meeting me halfway. He leaned down and pressed his lips to mine.

I wrapped my arms around his neck and absorbed the warmth of his kiss, enjoying the shivers that traveled along my arms. He smelled divine, like some sort of masculine soap and his own unique scent.

Finally, I pulled back. "We really need to work out some time off."

Over the last week, the most we'd managed were a few stolen hours for kisses and conversation. I was pretty sure I was ready to take it up a notch, but timing had not been working in my favor.

A grin tugged at the corner of his full lips. "As soon as you're not running for your life or trying to figure out what's coming for you, we'll work on it."

"Deal." I reached for his hand, and we started toward P & P. "Did you sort out the demon thing?"

"Another uprising," he said. "Again, they were gone by the time I got there."

"Like last week." He'd been called away for almost the exact same reason.

"Exactly, but in a different location."

"Think they are linked?"

"Could be. I'm not a fan of coincidences." He held open the door, and I preceded him inside. The shop was warm, and the rich scent of espresso and buttery pastry wafted toward me. Two regulars sat at their usual table, drinking coffee and reading the paper.

Connor hustled out of the back. His gaze brightened when it landed on us. "Got your stuff ready. Just finished the last batch."

"Thanks." I grinned, eyeing his band T-shirt. The Proclaimers. Classic. As if on cue, the song about walking 500 miles popped on over the speakers. I pointed to the little black box blaring sound. "This is one of my faves."

"I always knew you had good taste." He pushed the flop of dark hair off his forehead. "Can I get you a drink before you go? Espresso for both of you, right?"

"Exactly." I grinned.

"Yes, thanks," Roarke said.

Connor turned and set about fiddling with his fancy silver espresso machine. Roarke and I approached the counter. The glass display case was full of frosted, fruity confections and fat, fluffy muffins.

"Everything looks amazing," I said.

"Agreed." Roarke squeezed my hand. "That means you should get one of each."

I laughed. I wasn't usually a huge breakfast eater, but this morning I could do some serious damage to the contents of the display case.

After Connor passed over our espressos and packaged us up a few pastries to go, we paid and followed him toward the back. The narrow galley kitchen was immaculate, as usual. Almost like the pastries popped out of thin air, though I knew he'd been baking them since early this morning. When Connor slept, I had no idea.

At the far end of the kitchen, we waited outside the door to his potions shop. I peered in. As usual, it was cluttered and messy. Connor picked up two vials of bright green liquid and handed them to me.

"Careful," he said. "One drop of that touches your skin, and you'll be out like a light for half a day."

"Perfect." I held one up and watched the light glint through the potion. "So I just chuck this at him?"

"Yep. The glass is sturdy, but it will explode on impact and he'll be down for the count. And don't waste it. I only had enough ingredients for two. I can make more, but it'll take a week to get the supplies."

"What do we owe you?" Roarke asked.

"Just for the supplies," Connor said.

I examined Connor's workshop as Roarke paid him.

"Good luck," Connor said.

"Thanks, I think we might need it." I studied the vial in my hand. "Actually, we'll definitely need it."

When Roarke and I stepped out of the Underpath in Florida, the sun beat down harshly on our heads, a blazing light that heated my hair.

"Didn't this place get the message that it's winter?" I asked.

"Florida never gets the message."

We stood in a tiny graveyard in the middle of nowhere. Massive trees decorated with moss threw speckled shade everywhere except on us, and the battered old church at the edge of the cemetery looked like it had seen better days. There was as much bare gray wood as there was peeling white paint. Headstones tilted this way and that. And those were the lucky ones—most were toppled over entirely.

"This place was abandoned after the Depression," Roarke said.

"Not a surprise. There's nothing out here."

"Not anymore. Just the swamp." He pointed east.

I was about to ask how he knew it was that direction when the rumble of a car's engine broke the midday silence. A moment later, a battered red pickup truck with a white stripe trundled up in front of the church.

A demon wearing a cut-off flannel shirt and a John Deere cap hung out of the driver's window and shouted, "Hey, boss!"

"Your associate?" I asked.

"Jim Bob, the one and only."

"A backwoods demon?"

"Swamp demon. There's a difference, and he'll thank you not to forget it."

"Right-o." I followed Roarke across the uneven ground of the cemetery, dodging the tilted headstones.

"Thanks for meeting us, Jim Bob." Roarke reached out and shook his hand through the open window.

Jim Bob had a lump under his bottom lip that I could only assume was tobacco. He poked it with his tongue, then grinned. It wasn't attractive, though he was endearing in his own weird way. The only sign that he was a demon were the two little bumps under his hat where his horns would be.

"Not a problem, boss." Jim Bob had some kind of southern twang that I couldn't readily identify, but I assumed it was Everglades demon, if that was even a thing. "Hop in. I'll take you to the water. I got my airboat there, waiting for you."

We climbed in, Roarke in the front and me in the back. I had to clear out a space amongst the chewing tobacco containers and Pabst Blue Ribbon cans, finally crunching down into some sort of seat. I'd have to tell Cass—she'd approve of this demon's taste in beer.

Jim Bob peeled away from the church, his tires kicking up dust.

"Been a bit dry lately, but there'll be plenty of water in the swamp. Gators, too."

Oh, my favorite.

"Do you know anything about a settlement in the swamp?" Roarke asked.

"Yup." Jim Bob nodded. "Far back, past Picnic Island and deep into no-man's land. Humans can't go there."

"Can't or don't?" I asked.

"Both. It's a little supernatural settlement for runaways. Lawbreakers, mostly. Hiding out for their crimes. There's a spell that repels humans, but if you get too close, other things will keep you out."

"Anything we should be aware of?" Roarke asked.

"Yeah." Jim Bob leaned over and spat out the truck window. "Try to keep a low profile. Go to Willy's, the bar in town, and ask Willy how to find whoever it is you're looking for. But be prepared to pay."

"Willy owns the place?" I asked.

"Does indeed. He'll be behind the bar, slinging drinks."

He pulled the truck over to the side of the road where a long, calm river was bordered by a sea of tall grass that waved in the wind. The grass was planted firmly in the water, some kind of aquatic species. A weird little boat with a huge fan on the back idled in the water. It had a flat metal bottom and two seats up on stilts. There was also a seat for the driver, closer to the fan and up a bit higher.

Jim Bob pointed to the boat. "There she is, the Swamp Monster. My baby."

"It's beautiful," I said. It wasn't, not really. But he was so proud that I had to say it. And it was certainly interesting.

"Built it myself." He climbed out of the car and we followed. Jim Bob handed the keys to Roarke. "Head northeast and treat her good."

Roarke nodded. "Will do."

Jim Bob saluted and returned to his truck. The engine growled as he revved it, and he peeled off.

I looked at Roarke. "Ever driven one of these things?"

"No. But it can only carry three, and once we have Caden, we're at our limit, so I'd better learn."

"Yep." I stepped onto the boat. It rocked a bit, but was mostly stable. I'd take what I could get. If I didn't end up dunked in the swamp today, I'd consider it a win.

Roarke climbed on behind me and cranked the engine. The fan whirred to life, a loud roar that cut across the silent swamp. I climbed up into one of the seats, stripping off my jacket and laying it on the seat next to me.

Roarke took the captain's chair, turning the boat to head down the river. On either side, tall fields of grass waved in the wind. It was easily taller than my head. As we roared past, birds set off flying across the sky.

I'd Googled the Everglades last night and learned that it was called the River of Grass—one massive, slow moving body of water that was a mix of waterways, grassy aquatic fields, and mangrove forest. The boat skidded on the water as Roarke got the hang of the fan propulsion, and we set off.

"Turn right when you can!" I shouted, using my dragon sense to find the exact location of the settlement.

A few moments later, another small river appeared between the waving grass, and Roarke turned into it. The back of the boat swung around too far, but we made it in.

For hours, we threaded our way through rivers and fields of grass as the sun beat down and gators slithered out of the way of our boat.

"Feel that?" I shouted when the prickly sense of a protection charm raked across my skin.

"Must be getting close."

"Yeah."

Eventually, we made it into the mangroves. It was a thick forest of spindly trees with roots that grew right down into the water. They grew overhead, cutting out some of the bright sunlight. The waterway was barely wider than our boat, and Roarke slowed our progress.

"Weird place," Roarke said.

"Yeah." No sooner had the word left my mouth than the Mangroves began to close in on us. They picked up their roots like legs and walked into the middle of the waterway, blocking our progress. Weird magic shimmered on the air, feeling like bark against my skin and smelling...swampy.

It was the only way to describe it.

"Damn." I couldn't even see through them, they were so thick. "This is what Jim Bob was talking about."

"Which means there's probably no way around. Not if they protect the whole settlement."

I reached out with my magic, trying to get a feel for the mangroves. "Do you think they're alive?"

Roarke hesitated, clearly trying to get a feel for them the same way that I was. "As plants, yes. Like people, no."

"Okay. I'm going to try something. Be ready to move forward."

"Ready."

I sucked in a deep breath and called on my telekinesis. I'd practiced a bit last night, bending a spoon like any old hack in a movie, but this was a hell of a lot bigger. However, I also had a hell of a lot more at stake.

As the cool breeze of the Telenec demon's magic flowed over me, I envisioned the roots parting and allowing us through. Mentally, I moved them back the way they came.

Nothing happened.

The strain made my muscles tremble and sweat drip down my temples. My breath grew short as I pushed my magic toward the mangroves.

Finally, one shifted. It vibrated, then moved, picking up its roots and walking back to the edge of the waterway. One by one, the trees moved.

It took a lifetime. If something had been chasing us, we'd have been dead. Fortunately, it was just us, so my slow magic was fine.

The engine growled to life, and the whir of the fan blades broke through the silence. Roarke directed the boat through the mangroves as I continued to force them back, making a path for us.

By the time we reached the other side, I was sweating like mad and about to collapse.

"Good work," Roarke called over the sound of the fan blades.

"Thanks!" I gasped, trying to get ahold of myself.

The boat had motored into a large, open body of water. On one side, the fields of grass waved. On the other, massive trees hanging with moss dotted a patch of land.

"Can you feel the magic?" I asked. It prickled against my skin, different than a regular protection charm.

"Yes. This whole place is strange."

A massive gator stared at me impassively from the bank where it was sunning itself. The thing had to be fifteen feet long, if it was an inch. Another one popped out of the water only feet from the side of the boat, its eyes unerringly finding me.

"Hi," I said weakly.

Gators scared the hell out of me. Rightfully so. They were basically dinosaurs on tiny legs. And tiny limbs had never stopped a T-rex.

The gator just stared.

I waved. Did his mouth turn up in a grin? Hard to say, since it was terrifying.

I glanced back at Roarke. "Let's keep moving. Head north."

He nodded and directed the boat north. The sun was beginning to set, turning brilliant orange as it neared the horizon.

A few moments later, I held out a hand in the universal motion for stop.

Roarke cut the engine, and we drifted to a halt, the boat finally stopping when the bow brushed the field of grass.

"We're really close, I think. Let's wait till the sun sets. Keep a low profile."

"Agreed." Roarke pointed to a couple of paddles sitting in the hull of the boat. "We can approach with these."

"Perfect."

We stood silently, watching the sun dip down over the horizon. Deep shadow cut across the water and grass. Night bugs and animals began to screech and howl.

"I don't want to know what the heck else is out here besides giant gators," I muttered.

Roarke chuckled, but the sound was cut off by a rustling in the grass.

"Not the wind," I whispered, debating whether or not I should adopt my Phantom form. But my blue glow might shine above the grass, drawing predators toward us.

The rustling grew louder. Water splashed. My hair stood on end.

Out of the corner of my eye, I caught sight of the black tornado of Roarke's magic as he shifted to demon form. I drew my sword from the ether, powering up an icicle spear just in case I needed it.

Roarke finished the transformation and picked up an oar, propelling us backward from the grassy reeds. We were only five feet away when a massive form plunged through the grass.

It was easily twenty feet tall and covered in scraggly gray hair. A squashed face and beady black eyes completed the strange figure.

Bigfoot?!

I swung my sword toward him. He was too far away for me to make contact but he reached out one long arm and grabbed me around the waist like he was freaking King Kong. I stifled a scream as I struck out with my blade. It bounced off his thick hide, and he tucked me under his arm like a football.

The rotten cabbage scent of his fur made me gag. Bile rose in my throat as I struggled to free my sword arm. It was no use, so I flailed and kicked. Anything to make him drop me. But that was worthless too. I was tucked tightly against him as he trundled through the swampy reeds. Water splashed me with every step.

I called upon my Phantom form, letting the magic flow through me. My skin turned transparent and blue. I pushed against his side, willing myself to drift though him like I normally would. But nothing happened.

Dang it.

Whatever magic this monster possessed, it was blocking me. He was the ultimate predator—able to hold on to any prey.

Except I *really* didn't want to be prey.

An idea popped into my mind. I already had my ice magic powered up… I drew upon it. But instead of an icicle, I sent the icy magic down into the water at Swamp Thing's feet.

He roared, the sound echoing through the quiet night. I forced more magic into the water, straining to give it everything I had. His steps slowed. At least, I thought they did because I bounced less. I couldn't see anything because my head was pressed against his smelly side.

Finally, he stopped dead still and roared again, sounding like an enraged lion. I kicked, trying to free myself, but made no headway. A second later, the monster's arm loosened and I fell, crashing against the frozen swamp water. Pain shot through my hip.

Above me, Roarke flew at the monster's side. He must have pulled Swamp Thing's arm away from me.

From this angle, the beast definitely looked like Bigfoot, with his furry man-shaped form and apelike face. But Bigfoot was supposed to be a myth. Despite all the crazy species in the supernatural world, Bigfoot was still a mystery.

But if the big shoe fit…

Bigfoot swatted at Roarke, though he couldn't lunge toward him because his feet were still trapped in the ice. I was too familiar with his long reach. Roarke dodged, flying around to the beast's back. I recognized that move. He was going to break his neck.

"Stop!" I cried, guilt streaking through me. What if this *was* Bigfoot? I couldn't be responsible for his death. And he hadn't killed me. Maybe he was lonely and stealing me to be his Bigfoot bride?

"Stop?" Roarke's voice was gravelly, as it always was when he was in demon form.

"Don't kill him." I scrambled back across the ice, pushing my way through the grass that poked up. It scraped my hands. I dug into my pocket and pulled out one of the potion bombs.

Without a second thought, I hurled it at the monster. It crashed again his massive chest and exploded in a poof of green. The beast opened his mouth to roar, but no sound came out. Instead, his eyes rolled back in his head and he swayed, eventually falling backward like a massive oak.

He landed with a solid *thud* against the ice that I'd created, crushing the grass.

Roarke landed at my side. "What did you do that for? Don't you normally kill demons and monsters?"

I shrugged as I climbed to my feet. "Yeah, but doesn't he look like Bigfoot?"

"Bigfoot isn't real."

I pointed to the body. "Sure looks like he is."

Roarke studied the body. "You could be right."

"I think I am. There's so many supernatural creatures that it's crazy no one has ever proven the existence of Bigfoot. But here he is!"

"Take a picture."

I grinned and reached for my phone, then hesitated. I clenched my fist. "No. Let him stay a mystery. I don't want to be the one to ruin it for him."

"Then we'd better go. I don't know how long that potion will last on him."

"Good point." I hoped he woke up before the ice melted. Though he was so big and the water so shallow that I doubted he'd drown.

"Want a lift?" Roarke asked.

Freezing the water hadn't killed the grass—not yet, at least—and it grew up around me like a thick forest. Worse, the stalks were really sharp, with tiny teeth all along their serrated edges.

"Definitely, thanks."

Roarke picked me up, holding me against his chest. He flew over the tops of the grass, toward our boat that was now drifting back across the open expanse of water.

The view from up here was crazy. It was nearly dark now, but I could make out the sea of tall grass that waved in the breeze. Open waterways cut through the field as winding rivers and straight passageways. Here and there were patches of mangrove forest and little islands of land dotted with trees. In the distance, tin rooftops gleamed in the light of the moon and stars. The trilling chirp of crickets and frogs sent up a cacophony as they woke with the moon.

"We're close." I pointed to the roofs. "It's just over there."

"Good. It's dark enough to approach."

Roarke lowered us to the deck of the boat. It rocked underfoot, but I steadied myself against the tall seat. The sandalwood scent of Roarke's magic surged as he shifted back to his human form.

"To keep a low profile," he said.

"We'd probably better paddle our way in, then, huh?"

"Probably." He bent and picked up both sturdy paddles, then handed one to me.

We each took up position, him slightly ahead of me at the bow, and began to push through the water. The boat had such a shallow draft that it was easy to make quick headway through the calm water. Moonlight glinted off the jet-black surface, and the occasional ripple made me think of gators.

"Real swampy out here." The sounds of the crickets and frogs nearly drowned out my quiet voice.

"That's the truth."

We followed the water passageway through the reeds, turning left to come upon a big section of open water dotted with wooden houses hovering about three feet over the surface, built on thick wooden stilts. They were all ramshackle and rough-looking.

There were probably about fifty buildings, all laid out like a small town with streets and everything. Though the streets were made of water. Wooden porches surrounded each building, and airboats were pulled up alongside many of them. Though it was possible to walk from some buildings to another using the wooden porches that touched each other, many of them sat alone too. Golden light glowed through small square windows.

We paddled toward the entrance to town, which wasn't anything formal. Just the beginning of the water street. The sound of the crickets and frogs was muffled here, as if even they didn't dare get too close.

Dark magic prickled against my skin as we made our way between the buildings, down the narrow street. I shivered, unable to help myself. It felt a lot like Darklane, which was no surprise.

The twang of music filtered toward us, something that could only be described as a swamp jive. Lots of banjo. I liked it. Maybe they'd have a CD I could buy for Connor.

Or maybe that was nuts. We were hunting Roarke's evil brother in a dark magic town. There wouldn't be time for acting like a tourist.

The road turned onto a main thoroughfare. There were no other boats out, but it was wider and the buildings slightly larger. At the end of the street on the left was a larger building with lights glaring. Music poured from the open door.

"Twenty bucks, that's Willy's." I pointed with my oar.

"I won't take that bet. You'll win."

"Smart man."

We paddled toward it and turned down a small alleyway right before the main building. There was a line of airboats pressed up against the wooden walkway.

"Swamp parking lot," I muttered.

"Let's just hope that Jim Bob's airboat doesn't get keyed."

I grinned. "Better park inside the lanes, then."

"There are no lanes."

"A perfect analogy for this town." I stowed my oar and grabbed my jacket, slipping it on, then boosted myself up onto the wooden walkway. Roarke passed up a rope, and I tied off the bow of the boat to a post. I took the stern rope and finished the job, then Roarke jumped up and joined me.

"Try not to look so wholesome," Roarke said.

"Wholesome?" I looked down at my all-black leather. With my jet hair and pale skin, I didn't exactly look wholesome. That was for blonde girls in dresses.

"Compared to the folks in Willy's, you're going to look wholesome," Roarke said. "Scowl. Look a little drunk. We don't want to seem like threats."

"That, I can do." I leaned against his side and grabbed his arm, holding on like a drunken monkey. He was strong and warm against me, so it was no hardship to cling to him. I dropped my eyelids and slurred, "How's this?"

"Laying it on a bit thick, but it should do."

"Good." I didn't know how Roarke was going to try to look non-threatening—fact was, with his size, he really couldn't—but better to have just one of us look like a threat rather than two. And if he appeared to be distracted by my hot self instead of pinning people in his laser gaze, people would be less scared of him.

We ambled down the walkway, footsteps thudding on the dock, and around the corner. Music blared out the windows and door, which was swung open to the night.

A few people leaned against the rough wooden wall, swilling beer and staring out at the water. I ignored them, trying to maintain the illusion of a harmless drunk girl. Though drunk girls were rarely harmless, most men were blind enough to think they were.

We turned to go through the main door, and the scent of stale beer and sweat hit me hard.

"Looks like showering isn't a big thing here," I muttered.

"Clearly not."

The place was bigger than it looked from the outside, with a few dim bulbs hanging from the low ceiling. Dark shadows spread over the crowd, which was large and diverse, like the crowd at the gambling den.

A variety of magical signatures swept over me, everything from the smell of rotten eggs to a chill wind. Most of them were dark, the kinds of powers that hurt more than helped. No surprise, for a place that was a hideout for the worst of the worst in the supernatural community.

In the back corner was a three-piece band made up of individuals who looked like they slept in the swamp—literally *in* the swamp. Like, underwater. They had slimy green skin and weeds hanging off them. But damn, could they rock a tune. The one with the banjo was wailing on it, and honestly, I kinda wanted to dance. I didn't know *how* one danced to this music—probably a lot of knees and elbows—but it would be fun.

"I kinda like the band," I said.

"Me too. Surprisingly."

The rest of the crowd appeared to be huddled in groups. Card players in the front right corner of the bar, pool players at the left. Dancers in the back right near the band and mopers at the far left. The bar was pushed up against the far wall.

As we approached, I took in my surroundings, looking for threats. Folks were interested in us, with many peering our way, but no on looked like they were about to attack.

There was a tiny free space at the bar, and we squeezed in, right between a couple making out like they were going down on the *Titanic* and a massive monster who looked like a relative of the band. Though he was twice their size, he, too, dripped with weeds and green slime.

I pushed closer to Roarke, trying not to get any on my clothes. The smell of rotten vegetation was fierce, and I didn't relish smelling like that for the rest of this adventure.

Roarke leaned over the bar and caught the bartender's attention. Willy looked just like I would have expected—cut off T-shirt and denim shorts, a lack of dedication to oral hygiene, and a ball cap stuck on his head with the bill tilted up.

Willy leaned on the bar. "Yer not from around here, are ya?"

"You are, though," Roarke said.

"That, yer right." Willy chewed on a massive wad of something in his cheek. I had no idea what it was and didn't care to guess.

From behind the bar, mounted gator heads stared down at us impassively. I scowled. Dead animals shouldn't be decor. Even gators.

Roarke pitched his voice low. "We're looking for an old friend and were told you might be able to help."

"An old friend, eh?" Willy asked.

"Yes."

"That's what they all say." Willy stuck his hands in his pockets and leaned back on his heels. "It'll cost ya."

"That's fine."

"Meet me out back, then. Five minutes."

Roarke nodded.

We killed a few minutes at the bar. The swamp monster kept leering at me.

I scowled up at him. "Quit trying to look down my shirt, Swamp Thing."

"Not low enough to give a show, anyway." His voice sounded like gurgling water.

"That's the point."

"Can't keep a guy from hoping."

Roarke stepped around, as if he were going to try to defend my honor or something chivalric and old school. I pushed against his stomach, holding him back.

"I got this," I muttered to him. "And the last thing we need is a fight."

I turned back to Swamp Thing and smiled sweetly, then pressed my fingertip to his chest and shot some of my icy cold magic into him. His slime froze. "If you don't back off, I'm going to freeze your internal organs, turn them into ice cream, and then feed it to a gator."

I had no idea if I could selectively freeze his organs, but my magic was cold enough that Swamp Thing swallowed and nodded, backing up.

"That's right," I said. "You go on now. And have a nice night."

I gave a little wave of my fingers and he spun, headed for the hills. Or the swamp. Or whatever, as long as it was far enough from me.

"Nicely done," Roarke said.

"I know." I smiled up at him. "Nice thing about supernaturals is that big threats can come in small packages."

It was one thing I hated about the human world. The biggest guys could often throw around their weight and strength like it made them important. Problem was, it did. If you were too small to fight and didn't have a gun, then the big guy won. That left women at a real disadvantage. But here, in the supernatural world, I could kick as much ass as the biggest dude.

With Swamp Thing no longer causing problems, we turned to leave. The locals still eyed us, curiosity and annoyance on their faces. A shiver of foreboding went over me. I might be tough, but if *all* these folks decided I was bad news, then I was screwed.

We left the bar and followed the wooden porch around to the back. The orange glow of a cigarette waited for us, the only color in the otherwise black night.

"Are you sure it's a good idea to smoke when your house is made of wood?" I asked. "And there's gators waiting when it sinks?"

We were close enough that I could now see Willy shrug in the dim light of the moon. "So I smoke outside."

"I guess that helps," I said.

"I figure it does." He flicked the spent cigarette into the swamp.

"Not worried about littering?" I asked.

"Nah, Clarence loves the things."

A splash sounded, and I caught sight of a huge gator out of the corner of my eye. He'd chomped down on the cigarette butt with his massive jaw.

"You feed your pet gator cigarette butts?" Roarke asked.

"What? He likes 'em." Willy shrugged. "Now, what do you want to know?"

"We're looking for a man who looks a bit like me, but a bit shorter and paler," Roarke said. "He's part demon, with a magic that allows him to disappear at will into black mist."

A crafty gleam entered Willy's eye. "I thought you looked familiar."

"That means he's here, then?" I asked.

Willy nodded. "Sure does. But that information will cost you."

Roarke dug into his pocket and pulled out a wad of bills. He passed them over to Willy. "Will that do?"

Willy rifled through the stack with fingers so grimy I hoped he didn't serve food at his establishment. He tucked them into his back pocket and looked up, grinning. "Sure will. You'll find your guy at the far end of town to the east. Last building on the left as you exit town."

"You know anything else about him?" Roarke asked.

"Nope. Keeps to himself mostly. Moved in a while ago."

"Thanks." Roarke held out his arm for me. "Let's go, honey."

I took his arm, nodded goodbye to Willy, and followed Roarke down the boardwalk toward our boat.

"Honey?" I muttered.

"Keeping in character. But I think I like it."

"I suppose it's not the worst. Are we at cute-nickname phase, though?"

"I'd like to be."

I grinned. "Good enough for me. BooBear."

"Oh, I'm not sure about that one."

I laughed. "Okay, I'll think of something better."

"Less ridiculous, at least."

We reached our boat and hopped in. After untying the lines, we picked up the oars and pushed ourselves away from the boardwalk. Roarke steered us east, which was no easy feat, considering the boat lacked both rudder and keel.

The night was silent as we drifted through the darkened town, the sound of the swamp band fading as we reached the edge of the settlement. Crickets and frogs were loud enough out here to cover the noise of our paddles cutting through the water.

We drifted up to the last house on the left. Roarke grabbed the house's boardwalk and stopped our boat's forward trajectory. Quickly, I adopted my Phantom form, letting the cold magic flow through me. When I was fully transparent, I gestured between myself and the house, trying to indicate that I would sneak in and chuck the potion bomb at Caden.

Surprise was essential, and we didn't want him hearing our physical bodies climbing up onto the walkway.

Roarke nodded, and I climbed up onto the boardwalk, my Phantom form completely silent. I retrieved the potion bomb from my pocket and drifted toward the house wall. Though I wanted to peek in the windows, Caden might see my glow if I did that.

Instead, I knocked on my head, then drifted straight through the wall, my gaze darting around as I appeared on the inside of the sparsely decorated home. A figure lay asleep on the bed. Caden.

As if alerted by my presence, his eyes snapped open. He lunged for me, faster than anything I'd ever seen. One second he was on the bed, the next, he was on me.

CHAPTER THREE

I shuddered hard at the feel of his arms wrapped around me. Though he couldn't hurt me while I was in my Phantom form—in fact, he couldn't even make true contact—I felt his touch like I'd never felt anything before. I shouldn't have been able to feel anything at all in my Phantom form, but I did.

Bile rose in my throat at the slimy sensation that pulled at my soul. It coated me, giving my transparent blue skin a grayish cast. Panic beat in my chest, making my heart race. Somehow, he was hurting me. I didn't understand it, only that it felt wrong and disgusting.

I called upon my ice power, hurtling an icicle through his upper shoulder. It threw him back from me, pinning him to the wall. He shouted in pain, his dark eyes flaring with rage as he struggled to pull free.

Before he could, I hurled the potion bomb at him. It exploded in a flash of green against his chest. A moment later, he sagged against the wall, collapsing to the ground as the icicle snapped.

Roarke burst into the room as I hurried to Caden. I dug Cass's magic-dampening cuff out of my pocket and shoved it over his wrist. I squeezed the cuff so that the two ends almost met and then called on my new gift over metal. It flowed through me, hot and strong, and I pushed it into the metal. The ends of the cuff glowed bright orange before fusing together. It was tight enough that it would be impossible to remove without cutting it off, and it should work to dampen Caden's magic so he couldn't turn to mist and escape.

"What's wrong?" Roarke dropped to his knees at my side. "Your blue glow…"

"I don't know." It was still screwed up, slightly gray as well as blue. "But we need to stop this bleeding."

The wound in Caden's shoulder was weeping blood. He had information we needed—hell, he was Roarke's *brother*—so I couldn't let him die.

I scrambled to the bed and pulled off the covers, thrusting it at Roarke. "Tear off strips."

He rent the fabric. "Should we remove the icicle?"

I examined it, pushing back the fabric of Caden's ragged black shirt. It looked like the skin was already starting to mend at the edges. I lifted his shoulder and peered at the exit wound where the icicle had broken off. The skin had almost mended over the broken end of the ice.

"Yeah," I said. "He's got some kind of advanced healing. Pull out the icicle."

"That's a new talent," Roarke said as he pulled the icicle free, then wrapped the bandage around his brother's shoulder.

43

I sagged back, gasping. For fate's sake, this job was stressful. Give me a monster over long-lost family drama any day.

Roarke's face was unreadable as it traced his brother's sleeping form. I thought I saw sorrow there, but I couldn't be sure. Too many emotions flickered across his face.

"He should be okay now. Let's get him out of here and—"

Caden gasped and jerked upright, his gaze flying to Roarke.

What the hell? He was supposed to be out for hours. With that injury, he should *definitely* still be unconscious.

"Roarke," Caden growled.

"Brother."

Caden swung at Roarke, catching him in the side.

Roarke didn't flinch, instead reaching for Caden. But his brother was too fast. He scrambled up and darted away.

Panicked, I threw a blast of ice at Caden's feet. He skidded, arms flailing, and crashed to the floor. Roarke was on him a second later, trying to get him into a submission hold. But Caden slithered out, fast and strong despite his smaller size and injury.

They grappled on the floor, each trying to get the better of the other. Though Caden threw more mean shots—aiming for Roarke's groin and eyes—I kinda thought he wasn't going for the kill.

At least, I hoped he wasn't. Not that I thought he could get one over on Roarke, but that would just be too cruel, learning that your brother wanted to kill you.

Roarke could handle this, but we'd need a way to subdue Caden once he did. I turned in a circle, searching the room for weapons or any metal that I could make into shackles. If he was anywhere close to as strong as Roarke, rope certainly wouldn't do.

A quick inspection of the room revealed that there were no swords or daggers. What did Caden use for weapons, then?

In the kitchen, I found two heavy iron skillets. They weighed about ten pounds each, so they should do just fine.

The sound of a fist hitting flesh made me wince. I turned to see Roarke on top of his brother. He'd landed a blow to Caden's ribs, but Caden socked him in the face. Fortunately, Roarke recovered quickly.

I turned back to my task, leaving them to it, and put one of the skillets on top of the other. I didn't want molten metal dripping through the wooden floor.

As Roarke and Caden fought behind me, I touched a fingertip to the top skillet and forced my magic into it, envisioning a pair of shackles. The metal glowed red hot and melted, forming a puddle in the bottom skillet.

Shit.

This was hard.

I sucked in a ragged breath and tried to force the metal into a pair of joined circles. Slowly, it coalesced to form something like what I'd imagined. It was rough and terrible, but we'd probably be able to get Caden's wrists through them and then I could tighten them.

I did the same with the other skillet, creating a pair for his ankles. I had to work more quickly so the molten metal didn't melt through the wooden floor, but the practice with the wrist shackles helped. By the time the ankle cuffs were done, they'd only melted half into the floorboards.

Once they'd cooled enough to touch, I pried them out of the floor and spun around. Roarke had Caden on his front with his arms behind his back.

"Those are cuffs?" Roarke asked.

"Sorta."

I hurried over and knelt beside them. Caden thrashed and cursed. The scent of dark magic wafted from him, turning my stomach with the smell of rotten eggs. I shoved the metal circles over Caden's wrists, no easy task since they were joined together.

When his hands had slipped through, I fed my magic into the metal, tightening it. The only problem was that it turned red hot. Caden yelled as it burned him.

"Sorry!" I said.

Finally, they were tight enough. No matter how he strained—and boy, did he try— he couldn't get free of them.

"Good job," Roarke said.

"Bitch," Caden hissed.

Roarke shook him by the shoulder. "Manners, brother mine."

"Dick," Caden spat.

"Fair enough." Roarke shifted on Caden, and we locked his ankles into the shackles. He wouldn't be going anywhere fast in this getup.

"Now let's get out of here." Roarke hauled Caden upright.

As we were heading toward the door, it burst open. Four figures flooded into the room, all supernaturals of indiscernible demon species. Their magic was distinctly dark, a variety of putrid scents that made me gag.

"We thought you was suspicious," the biggest one rumbled. He wore a battered leather vest and was covered in a scattering of tattoos that looked to be three dimensional. His eyes flickered with a weird light.

"Just paying a visit to a friend." Roarke wrapped an arm around Caden, looking massive and scary. His dark eyes glinted with threat.

"That guy?" Tattoo-dude asked.

"Is that not obvious?" Roarke asked.

Tattoo-dude shrugged.

"We'll be on our way, then." Roarke nodded to the door, the gleam in his eyes clear. *Get out or I'll put you out.*

"We can't let you take one of our own," Tattoo-dude said.

"You didn't even recognize him a moment ago," I said. "I bet you don't even know his name."

"Don't need to know his name to know he's one of us."

They should probably have a talk with Willy about selling out their own, then. But I didn't want to rat out Willy.

Until the rat himself walked through the door.

"Jeez, Willy," I muttered. "You sell us info then sic your dogs on us?"

"Just sold you the info." Willy chewed on whatever was in his cheek. "Don't want you running off with one of our own."

"Too bad." Roarke let go of Caden, who toppled to the ground.

I took that as my cue, loading up with an icicle and shooting the nearest figure in the thigh. He howled and went down hard, thrashing. Roarke knocked out the demon closest to him while I sent an icicle through Tattoo-guy's thigh.

Since they were just trying to protect someone, I didn't necessarily want to kill them if I didn't have to. And it didn't take long to clear out our opponents. They were now sprawled on the ground, howling and bleeding.

Unable to help myself, I watched one, avarice growing in the pit of my belly. I didn't know what his power was, but I wanted it. More than anything, I wanted to sink to my knees at his side and pull his magic from him. Not necessarily for the magic itself, but to relive that sense of controlling my fate that I'd felt when I'd killed the Telenec demon back in the alley in Darklane. In the middle of all this craziness, that moment of control had felt good. *Really good.*

"Come on, Del. We've got to move." Roarke's voice snapped me out of my trance.

I shook my head, clearing the haze, and nodded. I really didn't want to kill any of these demons, no matter how good it might make me feel in the moment to be in control.

Roarke slung Caden over his shoulder, and we raced out the door. Only to stop abruptly at the sight of the entire crowd from Willy's staring right at us. Dozens of swamp boats surrounded Caden's house, each laden with enemies whose eyes were glued to us.

They didn't have pitchforks, but they really should have.

"What'd you do to Willy?" the nearest one called. He had the deep southern drawl of a true Florida boy, but he looked like a giant demon with massive black horns. It was disconcerting.

Behind them, our own airboat floated away from the house. Someone had cut the lines, and it was now twenty feet off and slowly migrating away.

Great.

"Can you fly us out of here?" I whispered.

"Can only carry one. Caden's a dense bastard."

Shit. We'd have to fight our way out. And the odds weren't awesome.

A great roar rent the night air from somewhere to the east. Tension sizzled through the crowd. My own hair stood on end. It was so loud and full of rage.

And familiar.

"The Skunk Ape!" cried a high-pitched voice.

Skunk Ape?

"Run!" cried another.

Airboat engines roared to life, the din cutting out the sound of the Swamp Ape's roar. Our opponents peeled out, airboats bumping into each other in their haste to head west.

"This isn't good," I muttered.

"We need to get to the boat," Roarke said.

I eyed the water. Gators were popping up here and there, their dark eyes riveted to the east. Loud splashing sounded, growing closer and closer. The gators were interested in the Skunk Ape. They were also creating a nice, and terrifying, bridge between me and the boat.

"Fly Caden over!" I cried. "I'll follow."

"I'll come back for you," Roarke said.

"Sure." I couldn't tell him my plan, because it was stupid. But we were also running out of time.

The black mist of Roarke's tornado swirled around him, and he took on his demon shape. He grabbed Caden and took off into the air, huge wings carrying them away.

As soon as they were airborne, I sucked in a deep breath. The rotten cabbage scent of oncoming Skunk Ape only solidified my commitment. We were out of time.

"Hey, gators!" I called. "Could you help me out? Just… Please don't eat me!"

A couple of them glanced my way, but they were more interested in the oncoming Skunk Ape. I didn't feel any menace coming off them, at least, so maybe they were down with my request.

I adopted my Phantom form, trying to ignore the fact that I was still slightly gray, and leaped off the wooden dock. I landed on the back of the first gator, but he hardly moved. Thank magic my Phantom form was weightless.

This was so nuts.

I jumped across their backs, occasionally getting a curious glance. But like the hellhounds, these scary beasts seemed to like me. Or at least tolerate me. They were just too damned interested in the Skunk Ape to pay me much mind.

"You idiot!" Roarke yelled.

"They can't bite me!" I cried as I jumped.

I was almost to the boat when I realized that there was a gap too big to cross. Crap!

But then, one of the gators swam around, filling in the space. I swore I saw a toothy grin on his face.

"Thanks!" I jumped onto him, then over to the boat, making it in by an inch. Caden lay in the hull of the boat, still bound and spitting mad.

"You're crazy," Roarke said.

"Start the engine." I turned and waved at the gators. A few glanced at me, and their expressions were definitely friendly, but they quickly looked back toward the east.

As the giant fan roared to life, the Skunk Ape broke through the darkness. The stench was even stronger than before, and bile rose in my throat.

Roarke peeled away, the boat skidding as we turned. I looked back toward the Skunk Ape. The gators had surrounded him, snapping and biting, almost like they were protecting the town.

The monster roared, trying to break through, but the gators held him back, snapping at his legs. Some of the reptiles were over fifteen feet long. I wouldn't want to trifle with them either.

The Skunk Ape's dark gaze met mine. I liked to imagine there was longing there, but I was probably just being ridiculous. Skunk Ape didn't want me for his bride. And I sure as heck didn't want to be his bride.

Either way, I needed to stop watching so many old horror movies.

We couldn't go through town or risk being followed by the locals, so Roarke steered us around the edge of the settlement and back toward safety. I kept an eye on Caden as we powered along, though he didn't look like he was going to make a run for it. Even with the grass, the whole swamp was basically water. Without the use of his limbs, he'd sink to the bottom and become gator food. And no one would want that fate.

It took us a couple hours to reach the bank where we'd left Jim Bob, but fortunately we didn't run into any more problems. The Skunk Ape had been too occupied by the gators to follow, and the townsfolk had given up.

Halfway there, Roarke called Jim Bob, who met us as we pulled up alongside the bank.

"That's a mighty disappointing prize you got there." He nodded to Caden.

"I'd have to agree," Roarke said, though I could tell in his tone that he didn't really mean it.

"Stinks something fierce too," Jim Bob said. "Black magic."

I nodded. "I thought I'd smelled that back at his place."

Caden's clothes weren't in great shape and he looked like it'd been a while since his last shower—a dunk in the swamp didn't count—but that wasn't enough to account for the smell. Jim Bob was right. It had to be black magic.

"Shut the fuck up, you fucking fuckwits," Caden growled.

"Eloquent," Roarke said.

Caden spit on him.

"This is going to be great," I said.

Roarke shot me a sardonic smile, the corner of his mouth curved up. For fate's sake, he was handsome. Even in these crappy circumstances and speckled lightly with swamp water.

Jim Bob pulled his truck around while Roarke hauled Caden out of the boat and tossed him in the back seat.

"Sit in front, Del." Roarke climbed into the back with Caden.

"I don't know what the fuck you want with me," Caden growled.

"You can't begin to imagine?" Roarke asked.

In the rearview mirror, I saw Caden snarl. Oh, he was a charmer, all right. Roarke had clearly gotten all the charm and saved none for his brother.

While Jim Bob drove us back to the cemetery, I called Mordaca and Aerdeca and asked them to meet us at Roarke's place. We wanted to question Caden, and the best folks to help with that were always the blood sorceresses.

After I hung up the phone, I twisted around and inspected the metal cuffs binding Caden. I could only see the ones at his ankles since his wrists here hidden behind his back. It was hard to say if they looked strained, but better safe than sorry, so I dialed Nix.

"Hey," I said when she picked up. "Do we still have that super strong chain?"

"The one that Roarke tore off like it was cotton?"

"That's the one."

"Yeah, we have it. Need it?"

"Yes. Bring it to Roarke's in an hour if you can."

"Perfect. Shop will be closing right around then. I'll see you there."

"Thanks!"

"Don't you think that if Roarke could tear that chain off, I could too?" Caden spat from the back of the car.

"Maybe," I said. "But I doubt it. He's stronger than you."

"Not by much."

Given how quickly he'd shaken off the effects of Connor's potion, I had to admit he was right. "Well, it's a good thing you're wearing the iron cuffs, then."

I called Connor for good measure, requesting some kind of sedative potion to weaken the muscles. He agreed to pass one off to Nix before she came over.

It was situations like these—weird, dangerous situations involving kidnapping, alligators, and Skunk Apes—that made me appreciate how amazing my family and friends were. They always had my back, and they had the weird talents to make every job easier. Worry still tugged at me—I had a feeling the worry was here to stay—but I could get through this. I *had* to get through this.

I might be some kind of Queen of Hell, but my life here on Earth was pretty dang great. I'd just have to work hard to make sure it stayed that way. And figuring out what the hell Caden knew about my role in the Shadows' plans was key.

CHAPTER FOUR

A couple hours later, Roarke and I waited in the foyer of his house. Outside, the sun was setting through the trees, casting a brilliant orange glow on the scatter of leaves. We were waiting for Aerdeca and Mordaca to arrive. If I turned back to the living room, I could see Caden bound in a chair with Nix, Cass, and Aidan standing guard over him.

I reached for Roarke's hand and squeezed. The movement made the faintest smell of rotten eggs waft up toward my nose. I'd been desperate to wash off the stink of swamp water and Skunk Ape, so we'd showered as soon as we'd gotten Caden all bound up.

However, I still kind of smelled. I tried to subtly get a better whiff, and it revealed more of the same.

That couldn't be good.

And of course Roarke smelled great with his masculine soap and the sandalwood scent of his magic. I glanced up to see him gazing out the window, his brow creased.

"You okay?" I squeezed his hand again.

"Fine."

"Fine?" That was a lie if I'd ever heard one. "You sure? Because you don't look fine."

He frowned, his gaze sad. "No, you're right. I'm not fine." He hiked a thumb back toward the living room. "That's my brother in there. My *brother*. And he's nothing like I remember. Whatever he's been doing these last ten years has changed him entirely."

"Yeah. Not for the better."

"No. I loved him once. Which makes this so much worse."

"And now? Do you love him still?" Because if that was the case, this had to be tearing Roarke up inside. His brother had sided with the Shadows, who were evil incarnate.

Roarke sighed. "I think I might. I'm not sure that kind of thing goes away, no matter what happens. You still remember the good times, and it keeps you going. Keeps you loving even when you know you shouldn't."

My heart clenched in my chest, a visceral pain. So strange how that could happen.

"I think I know how you feel." My new memories of my family were all pretty much horrible. Poking at them hurt like hell. It made sweat break out on my upper lip and my stomach turn. But I was compelled to speak. Because I did know how Roarke felt, and if it could help him, then I owed it to him.

"I know how you feel," I repeated. "I feel the same about my family. My mother and father were terrible. They locked me up to force me to learn my magic, they promised me to some kind of demon uprising, and they sold me to the Monster."

"They were truly awful." He squeezed my hand.

"They were. But still... I remember being little and loving them. I didn't know any better. They were my parents. Any affection that they showed me, I ate it up." I sucked in a ragged breath, remembering the dreams I'd been having this last week. Nice dreams. False dreams. "I created a mythology around them—who I wanted them to be. I think I may have even created positive memories from daydreams of the family I wanted to be part of."

At least, that was what I thought was happening. I had a feeling a therapist would confirm that was what I was doing. I'd have to ask Draka when I saw her again if the positive dreams were real. They probably weren't.

I shook my head, trying to clear it. "Anyway, I guess my point is that I understand where you are coming from. It's almost impossible to let go of family, even when they tear themselves away from you. But you can create your own family."

His dark gaze met mine. "Like you did with Nix and Cass."

"Exactly. You can do the same."

"I think I might be."

The seriousness in his eyes made me swallow hard. Did he mean me? I wasn't able to ask. The sound of a jet engine landing in the front yard stole our attention.

We turned to look out the window. A black muscle car—a Mustang, from the looks of it—pulled into the driveway. The paint job was custom—a glittering black that sparkled in the rays of dying sunlight. The engine had to have been modified, because it was louder than any car I'd ever heard.

The driver's door swung open, and Mordaca stepped out, her black bouffant hair appearing seconds before the rest of her. For the first time, she wasn't dressed in her plunging Elvira dress. Instead, she wore a black leather racing suit. Which plunged just like the Elvira suit did.

I grinned. You could always count on Mordaca to steal the show.

Aerdeca climbed out a moment later. She was dressed in her usual sleek white pantsuit with her fall of silver blonde hair gleaming in the dim light. Both sisters carried leather bags that looked like old-fashioned doctor bags. Of course Mordaca's was black, and Aerdeca's was white.

Mordaca stalked to the door; Aerdeca glided.

Roarke opened it just as they mounted the stairs.

"This house call will cost you." Mordaca's smoky voice was trailed by Aerdeca's light chuckle.

"Thank you for coming," Roarke said.

"No guarantees we can help." Aerdeca's blue gaze snapped to Roarke. "Though you'll still pay the fee."

"That's fine." He stepped back to let them in.

They glided past, the scent of their matching dark, smoky perfumes wafting by. Mordaca's nose twitched as she passed me.

Mordaca pointed down the hall to the living room. "That way?"

"Yes," Roarke said.

We followed them to the living room where Caden sat, bound to a chair. Aidan stood behind him, hand on his shoulder, while Nix and Cass watched from the couch.

"Isn't he a sight?" Aerdeca said.

I had to agree. Caden still wore the golden magic dampening cuff, the iron shackles, and now the massive chain that we hoped would help. He was also slumped over in his chair thanks to the sedative that Connor had given us. For now, we had him pretty well bound, but I wasn't sure it would last.

"Long time no see, Elvira," Nix said.

Mordaca grinned. "I'll take that as a compliment."

"I thought you might."

Mordaca and Aerdeca walked around to the front of Caden's chair. Roarke and I followed. I took up a spot near Cass and Nix.

Cass leaned over and whispered, "You doing okay?"

"Yeah."

"You sure? You look a little peaky."

"I'm okay." I squeezed her hand once to reassure her, though I could tell it didn't work.

"So what are we here for?" Mordaca asked. "Questioning?"

"Yes," Roarke said. "We need some information from him."

"Didn't want to try good old-fashioned torture?" Mordaca asked. "It'd be cheaper."

Roarke grimaced. "I'd prefer truth serum or something equally painless."

Aerdeca shrugged. "Your dollar."

"And we're happy to take it." Mordaca's blood-red lips curled up. It was almost a grin.

Aerdeca turned to Caden and knelt by the chair.

"What are you doing?" Roarke demanded.

The concern was clear in his voice. No matter what had happened with his brother, he didn't want Aerdeca or Mordaca hurting him.

Aerdeca glanced over her shoulder at him. "Just trying to get a feel for his magic. Different species do better with different truth serums. What are his powers?"

"He's part demon, like me. Though he now has the ability to disappear into mist, extreme speed, and also healing."

"Now has?" Mordaca asked. "He didn't have those before?"

"No."

Aerdeca leaned closer to Caden, her nose wrinkled as she sniffed delicately. "He stinks."

"Dark magic," Roarke said. "He's a practitioner."

"So are we, occasionally," Aerdeca said. "And we don't stink like that."

"While dark magic can smell bad, it doesn't always," Mordaca said. "I'm going to need to take some of his blood."

"For what?" Roarke asked.

"Literally anything that I do." She pointed to herself. "Blood sorceress here, remember?"

I reached out for Roarke's hand, feeling the tension in his grip. It was tearing him up to see Caden like this. And I had to admit, Mordaca was creepy. I trusted her, but if she was looming over one of my loved ones with her bloodthirsty magic, I'd be a bit jumpy, too.

"Fine," Roarke said. "Do what you must."

The room was silent as Aerdeca and Mordaca set about their work, opening their doctors' bags and removing bowls, vials, and a silver knife.

As they'd done with me when they'd helped me recover my memory, they worked as a team. Mordaca held the bowl beneath Caden's arm as Aerdeca made an incision. His blood dripped into the small stone basin. Once it was half full, they removed it.

Before Aerdeca could put a binding on Caden's wrist, the wound began to close. It was easy to see how he'd survived my ice pick to the shoulder. His wounds closed within minutes.

"Interesting," Aerdeca murmured. She rose to join Mordaca, who stood in front of us.

Mordaca held out the bowl, and Aerdeca opened three different vials, each filled with a different powder. She sprinkled a bit of the green one into the bowl of blood before moving on to the red and then blue. Then she stirred it with the silver dagger and struck a match, tossing it in.

The smoke that poofed up was black and oily, smelling strongly of rotten eggs. Mordaca grimaced, then turned to us. "You have a problem. A big one."

"What?" Roarke demanded.

"This man is cursed."

"Cursed? How so?"

"I believe it is an Influenta Curse, though which one, I do not know. There are many types. It makes him susceptible to the control of others."

My gaze darted to Roarke, though he was still staring at Mordaca. Did this mean that Caden hadn't wanted to side with the Shadows?

"How long has he been cursed?" Roarke asked.

"Oh, a good decade, at least," Mordaca said.

"A decade?" Roarke's voice was rich with shock. "No, I would have noticed. A decade ago he seemed normal. Now, he's…"

"Different," I finished for him. "Very different."

"Of course he is," Mordaca said. "Like all magic, the curse is decaying. It's why he stinks of rotten eggs. And why he's been behaving more erratically."

"It's a powerful magic," Aerdeca said. "But he is strong, too. His mind fights it, which makes the magic decay faster. Also, the curse may not have been made for his species."

"So he could just shake it off?"

"I'm afraid not." Mordaca frowned. "I don't know much about this particular type of Influenta Curse, but with magic as strong as this, it won't let go easily. He will continue to become more erratic, his behavior a threat to himself and others. Eventually, it will get him killed."

"So, we cure him. You can do that." Roarke didn't phrase it as a question.

"Actually, no," Aerdeca said. "I don't even know which Influenta Curse this is. It's part of the family of curses meant to manipulate others, but without knowing the origin, I can't find a cure."

Roarke shoved a frustrated hand through his hair, his gaze pained. He'd thought his brother was lost to him, then he'd been given a brief glimpse of hope. Now it'd been snatched way. "There has to be *something* we can do."

"Do you know anyone who might know more?" Aidan asked from his position behind Caden, who was still sedated. Connor had really brought out the big guns for this sedative, considering how poorly the last had worked.

"I don't," Mordaca said. "We are the best for a reason. The downside is that if we don't know, then no one does."

"That doesn't mean we can't still look," I said.

Roarke nodded gratefully to me. "And we will. But first"—he turned to Mordaca—"can you at least question him? We need information from him."

How quickly he switched from his desire to save his brother to his desire to save me. Roarke was nothing if not practical.

"We can try." Aerdeca frowned. "But it's likely to be difficult. The curse has messed with his mind. And if the information has anything to do with those who cursed him, he likely won't be able to give it up. No matter how strong our potions."

Made sense. If you were going to curse someone to make them help you, you wouldn't let them spill the beans about your plot.

Heart aching, I left Cass and Nix and walked toward Roarke, who stood near Mordaca and Aerdeca. When I reached him, I took his hand.

Mordaca's nose twitched again, and her gaze swung to meet mine. "You smell."

"Um."

She stalked closer, then sniffed deeply, then stepped back. "Oh, I thought I smelled something weird when I came in."

Aerdeca stepped closer and sniffed me, as well. I was about to push her back when she retreated and met Mordaca's gaze. Worry painted her features.

My stomach knotted.

"We're going to need some of your blood," Mordaca said.

"Her blood?" Roarke demanded.

"Her blood." Aerdeca turned and retrieved a fresh knife and bowl.

Dread curled in my belly, like I'd eaten a bad burrito.

"You think she's cursed," Roarke said.

"I can't say." Aerdeca returned with the knife.

I stuck out my arm and clenched my jaw.

"Sorry, this will sting." Aerdeca sliced the blade over my wrist.

Pain flared briefly, and I tilted my limb so that the blood dripped into the bowl. Though I was no stranger to blood, watching it pour out of me made my stomach turn.

When she'd decided she had enough blood, Aerdeca withdrew the bowl. Mordaca handed me a clean white cloth, which I pressed to the wound while I watched the blood sorceresses complete the ritual with the powders and the match.

A light sweat broke out on my skin as I waited. When the oily black smoke poofed up from the surface of my blood, I swallowed thickly.

"What does this mean?" Roarke's voice was hard.

"I'm not sure." Mordaca met my gaze. "Do you have any idea how this might have happened? Curses aren't contagious. But you have the same curse that he does."

"When I ambushed him earlier today, he lunged for me." I hesitated, but I could count on Aerdeca and Mordaca to keep my Phantom secret, so I pressed on. "I was in my Phantom form, so he couldn't grab me. But it felt…gross. Normally I feel nothing in my Phantom form, but this was different."

"In your Phantom form?" Mordaca glanced at Aerdeca. Something was clearly exchanged, though I had no idea what. "Will you show us?"

I suddenly felt a bit like a circus performer, but anything to get to the bottom of this, right? With a deep breath, I called on my Phantom form, letting the cool magic flow through me.

From behind, Cass and Nix gasped.

"Do you normally look like that?" Mordaca asked.

I glanced down at myself, horrified when I caught sight of the gray tinge to my transparent blue skin. It hadn't gone away. I'd thought it was a fluke, and I'd been so distracted that I just let it slip my mind.

Every cell in my body felt like it vibrated. My breath grew short.

"What does this mean?" Roarke repeated his question from earlier, his tone hard as rock.

Mordaca frowned. "It may be good. In a way. We can diagnose it, at least. The curse attached to Del in her Phantom form is a Phantom curse. There's only one Influenta Curse from a Phantom culture. You could get the cure from them."

Aerdeca touched Mordaca's arm. "No, they can't. That culture has been dead a thousand years."

"That won't stop Del."

Shock socked me in the stomach. Mordaca shouldn't know about my gift for bringing back the past. "How do you know that?"

"I have my ways. And you have yours. If you're lucky, those people will have a cure. You can bring their healer back from the past and beg, bribe, or steal a cure."

It might work. But I'd have to be sure to send the healer and her culture back to her own time when we were done.

"Where do they live?" Roarke asked.

"High in the Andes Mountains. They're a Phantom branch of the Inca called the Incate."

"Phantom branch?"

"Yes. A rare breed that are half-bloods, allowing them to be sentient."

Like my people. "That's a rare breed of supernatural."

"Yes. There have been a few settlements around the world. One in Wales, this one in Peru, another in China."

I didn't mention that *my* people were the Welsh Phantom half-bloods. The World Walkers, as they were called. Though I wondered if these Incate were World Walkers, too, I didn't ask. The cure was more important now, and I didn't want to reveal too much about myself.

"What do you know about these Incate?" I asked.

"They died out about four hundred years ago after contracting an illness from the Spanish Conquistadors. It was a rare strand of smallpox that could infect Phantoms."

"Freaking colonialists," Nix muttered.

"In fairness, our people did it to the Native Americans here," Aerdeca said.

"Yeah, we're jerks, too, with our smallpox blankets and Trail of Tears." Nix sighed, dejection clear in the sound. "Do you know where to find the Incate?"

"Not exactly, no. You'll have to find them," Mordaca said. "Which won't be easy. They lived in a mountain settlement, similar to the famous human settlement of Machu Picchu. They had an impressive array of protections guarding their home, which allowed them to hold out against the Spanish as long as they could, but they didn't last."

"So we have to get past whatever guards their settlement," Roarke said.

Aerdeca nodded. "And pray they can give you a cure."

"What if they can't?" I asked.

Mordaca glanced back at Caden, who was starting to shift as if he were coming to, and pointed to him. "That."

I swallowed hard. "Whoever is controlling him— could they control me, too?"

It meant I'd fall right into the Shadows' hands— forced to do whatever they wanted me to do.

"Perhaps," Mordaca said. "You weren't cursed in the same way that he was. His was deliberate. I don't understand the intricacies of your situation. The way the curse attached itself to you—it's strange, though not unheard of. You'll have to see if you can find out more from the people who created the curse."

"We just have to find them," I said.

"And that's the tricky part," Mordaca said.

CHAPTER FIVE

An hour and a half later, the kitchen looked like the study hall of the local college. Books and laptops were scattered across the kitchen table, with me, Nix, and Cass spread out and researching the Incate.

Roarke and Aidan sat in the living room, scouring the internet on two sleek laptops while keeping an eye on a sedated Caden. Guards would be coming by later, some of Roarke's demon minions, but until then, we didn't want to let Caden out of our sight.

After Aerdeca and Mordaca had collected their payment and left, we'd gotten lucky. Our dragon senses had latched onto the rough location of the Incate in the Andes Mountains in Peru. We knew the general direction of where to go, and our dragon senses would really light up once we arrived. The question was more about what we'd face when we got there and what the Incate would want in payment for the cure.

If they had one.

We might only have one shot at this, and we wanted to get it right—especially the payment part. Their culture was over five hundred years old. They wouldn't want cash.

Since we wouldn't be leaving until tomorrow morning, we'd decided to use this time to research.

Once again, books to the rescue.

We read, the three of us flipping pages quickly as we searched old treatises for explorers' accounts of their trading expeditions to visit the Incate. They were masters of booby traps protecting their settlements, the explorers wrote, but we hadn't yet found what trade goods they preferred.

With every page that I turned that didn't give me what I sought, the worry grew larger in my mind. It was like a great, hulking beast, growing fatter with every minute. Though the kitchen was bright with warm light and I was surrounded by friends and family, the darkness outside seemed to press in on the windows.

It was so much easier to be afraid at night, and this curse had hit me out of the blue.

Nix reached out, grabbing my hand. "It's going to be okay."

I looked up, meeting her gaze. Worry and love were clear in her blue eyes.

"You can tell I'm stressed?" I said. Anxiety was a noose around my neck.

"Who wouldn't be?" Cass said. "This is your second curse in less than a month."

"That is more than normal," Nix said.

Though curses weren't uncommon—far from it, considering that it was a major magical tool—two this close together was really bad luck.

"Yeah, I'm worried." Understatement. I squeezed Nix's hand. "It's just that if this is a curse from the Shadows, which I think it is, that means I'm susceptible to their suggestion. I wasn't worried about resisting their call to be their queen, but now…"

"If you're not in control of your own actions, then you've got a problem," Cass said.

"Exactly." It was like my worst nightmare, times one thousand. Part of me wanted to run out of here and find more evil demons and steal their powers, just so I could feel in control and build my arsenal. "And I can't help but wonder if this was a trap."

"Trap?"

"Yeah. They can't find me because of my concealment charm. But if they've learned of my connection to Roarke and know that he would hunt his brother…"

"Then they use Caden as bait," Nix finished. "Once you find him, he's like a sneaky bomb meant to detonate and hit you with his curse."

"Oh, shit," Cass breathed. "That's bad. And a real Hail Mary of a plan."

"Makes sense, though," I said. "They failed with Draka, but learned about Roarke and me when they captured us last week in Germany. Now they're scrambling for a new plan."

"It's a good one," Cass said. "Using your connection to Roarke is smart."

"Yeah." I sighed. "We're playing right into their hands. They know more than we do, and they set a trap that I walked into."

"You had to help Roarke save his brother," Nix said. "That's what we do."

"And the Shadows know that." I scrubbed a hand through my hair. "It's not that I regret helping Roarke. Of course not. I regret that I didn't think about this more. The Shadows are strong and smart. If they set this trap, it means I'm up against more than I realized."

"You'll beat them," Cass said.

"She'll only beat them if we keep researching," Nix said. "We need to know what the Incate are going to want in exchange for a cure."

"If there is one." Dread clutched at my stomach.

Cass gripped my hand hard. "There will be one. We will work this out."

"Worse has tried to get you than this," Nix said. "You came back from the freaking dead."

I laughed weakly, though my stomach still felt a bit off. Dying wouldn't be so bad compared to becoming a pawn of the Shadows, a tool to be used in their horrible plot. Whatever that was.

"I vow it on my PBR." Cass grinned.

This time, I actually laughed.

"You know she means it, now," Nix said.

"Thanks, guys." I squeezed each of their hands. With them at my back, this was possible. We'd been through worse, right?

Before I could dwell on it, the doorbell rang.

Cass jumped up. "Food!"

"Perfect." Nix stood. "We'll eat, refuel, then hit the books again."

"Good plan." My stomach grumbled, hunger replacing the worry that had soured it earlier.

We went out into the living room in time to see four massive demons enter, each carrying a big paper bag that smelled like Chinese food.

I joined Roarke and smiled at him. "Guards *and* delivery service?"

"Can't beat it," he said, then went to greet the guards. He handed off the bags to us, then gave them directions about watching Caden.

Nix, Cass, Aidan, and I returned to the kitchen, unloading the bags. There were at least twenty white cartons with the familiar red script, along with a few handfuls of fortune cookies.

"China Palace!" Nix said. "My fave."

Roarke entered. "I ordered a little bit of everything."

"Perfect." I hunted through the loot and found a carton of my favorite—Szechuan veggies. I stuck it next to the microwave, then poured myself a mug of red wine from the stash that Roarke kept just for me. Armed with my cup and my carton, I returned to the table.

Cass joined me, her usual PBR in one hand and a container of General Tso's chicken in the other. She'd always had the palate of a frat boy. She sat next to me and shoveled in a mouthful, an expert with chopsticks.

She chewed happily. "Perfect."

While Aidan and Roarke demolished six miscellaneous containers each, Nix squirted about a gallon of hot sauce into her spicy pork.

"I don't know how you don't have steam coming out of your ears," I said.

"I'm *caliente*." She grinned. "It just absorbs into me."

I smiled back. "You guys are the best, you know that?"

"Yeah, we know," Nix said.

"But so are you." Cass pointed her chopsticks at me. "Now eat up because we've got a big job ahead of us."

Around midnight, we finally found our answer. With the carcasses of white paper cartons scattered around, Nix held up a treatise written by a female trader in the eleventh century.

"They like obsidian!" Nix cried. "It says so, right here. Emisia the Bold visited them in 1025 AD to establish trading relations with her village on the other side of the continent. The treasure that the Incate were most interested in was obsidian."

"Volcanic glass?" Cass asked. "Like my daggers."

"Exactly," Nix said. "But ideally the rarer colors. Reds and greens, not black."

"At least we know what they like," Roarke said. "This was getting dire."

"I have a colleague who collects rare rocks," Aidan said. "I'll give him a call. We can have something ready for you by tomorrow morning, hopefully."

"Thank you." I smiled at him. Damn, it was good to have friends like these.

"Perfect," Roarke said. "Just tell me what I owe you."

"Don't worry about it," Aidan said.

"I insist." Roarke's voice was firm.

Aidan smiled. "We'll work it out."

Before they could get into a fight over who would pay—though I couldn't help but appreciate two generous guys—I stood. "Now that we have that answer, I need another shower and to hit the hay."

"You really don't smell like rotten eggs anymore," Nix said.

"I kinda feel like I do." I grimaced.

"It's dissipated," Cass said. "I swear on my PBR."

"Be that as it may, I'd feel better with a shower." I met each of their gazes in turn. "Thanks for the help."

"Always," Cass and Nix said in unison.

We split for the night, Cass, Nix, and Aidan heading back to town. Guards were going to keep an eye on a sedated Caden while Roarke and I got some sleep. They'd moved him to a windowless room in the basement—less opportunity for escape.

I went upstairs with Roarke. At the top of the landing, I turned to him. "I'm just going to shower, okay?"

"You really don't smell," he said.

"I know. Cass wouldn't have sworn on her PBR if she didn't mean it. But you have a pretty sweet shower, so I'm going to make use of it."

He leaned down and kissed me. I clung to him for a moment, enjoying the warm press of his lips, then pulled away.

It didn't take me long to shower. Though I wanted to linger in the enchanted grotto that Roarke had going on in the guest bathroom, I wanted to see him more. So I hurried out, rubbed myself dry, and took a good whiff.

My muscles nearly sagged in relief. I didn't smell.

With hope a bright light in my chest, I adopted my Phantom form. Just to check.

Unfortunately, I was still vaguely gray.

So, still cursed.

But at least I didn't smell. And we had a plan.

I dropped my Phantom form and drew in a breath, trying to banish the queasiness—we could handle this, we *would* handle this—then pulled on a robe and hurried toward Roarke's bedroom.

The hallway was dim and quiet, but warm light glowed from Roarke's room at the end of the hall. When I entered, he was standing with his back to me, looking down into a dresser drawer. The dresser was massive, like the rest of the furniture, but it fit well into the large bedroom. Mountain-chic, like the rest of the house.

Roarke turned, a smile on his face. "Feeling better?"

"Yeah."

My gaze riveted to the small box in his hand. "What's that?"

He glanced down at it, then held it out. "For you."

"A present?"

"Yes."

I smiled and approached, then reached for the small black box that was about four inches square. A jewelry box? I'd never been a big fan of diamonds and pearls.

I cracked it open to reveal the ugliest bracelet I'd ever seen. It was made of rough black beads, all misshapen and weird. My heart leaped and I gasped.

"Is this what I think it is?" I touched it reverently.

"If you think it's a lucky charm made by the fae of Ireland, then you are correct."

"Oh my gosh." I glanced up. "How did you find this? This is the bracelet of Eire. One of the luckiest charms in the world. I thought it was owned by some Russian billionaire."

It was like the Hope Diamond of lucky talismans. One of a kind and exceedingly valuable. I made a point to keep up to date with the most famous lucky objects. For the most part, I stuck to quantity rather than quality when it came to lucky charms. But this…this was quality.

"It was," Roarke said. "But he could be persuaded."

I arched a brow. "Not persuaded in the same way you persuaded the Kings of Hell to follow your rules, right?"

He laughed, then looped an arm around my neck and pulled me in for a brief kiss. "No. Persuaded in the normal way. With some begging and cash."

"I didn't realize you believed in lucky talismans."

"I'm still not sure about them, but you like them, so…"

I grinned, then stood on my tiptoes and pressed a kiss to his lips, speaking against them. "You are the *most* thoughtful man."

He wrapped an arm around my waist, pulling me tight against him.

I kissed him hard. He groaned and sank his hands into the damp strands of my hair. I softened the kiss, reveling in the taste of him as I ran my hands over his strong chest.

He pulled away and kissed a line down my neck, biting lightly at the slope where it met my shoulder.

I gasped. "I want you."

"All of me?" he murmured.

"Everything." My mind spun with images of what was to come. I wanted it all. After everything we'd been through, now was the time. I couldn't wait any longer.

He dropped to his knees, parting the robe above the sash and letting his lips hover over my skin. The heat of his breath sent a shiver racing through me. I ached for his touch.

"Please," I begged.

When his tongue darted out to trace a circle around my belly button, I sank my fingers into his hair and closed my eyes, transported by the pleasure of his touch.

"You taste amazing," he murmured.

"You *feel* amazing."

"Just you wait." He nipped at my skin and I gasped. "This is nothing. The best is yet to come."

CHAPTER SIX

Though we hadn't slept as much as we should have—for obvious and amazing reasons—we woke early the next morning. We were unsure of how long it would take to find the Incate, so we'd planned on an early start.

But when the alarm rang, I was deep in dreamland, reliving everything Roarke and I had done the night before. I groaned and rolled over, meeting Roarke halfway. His hair was mussed and his eyes sleepy, but he was so handsome that it hurt my heart to look straight at him.

"Morning." His voice was rough. If we'd had time, I'd have jumped on him again.

"Morning." I pressed a kiss to his lips, savoring him for the briefest moment.

Before I could forget the importance of today's mission and toss our plans aside, I pulled away.

"We'd better get going," I murmured.

"Agreed. Big day ahead."

Yeah. Huge day. We had to get a cure to this curse, or...

I didn't even want to think about it.

We climbed out of bed, and we showered quickly in separate bathrooms. After I climbed out, I pulled on fresh clothes. By the time I made it downstairs, Cass had arrived. She was sitting at the counter, drinking a coffee, with two black backpacks on the counter next to her.

"Roarke is downstairs, checking on Caden," she said.

"Thanks." I nodded at the backpacks. "That's the obsidian?"

"Yep. An assortment of red and green, with a bit of black as filler. The small pocket on your bag contains potions from Connor. Translation, tonics. Drink them before you have to speak to the Incate healer. You'll be able to communicate with her even though you don't speak her language." She dug into her pocket and pulled out a small black stone, which she held out. "Even better, Aidan found a transportation charm."

"Oh, perfect." I took it. "You're a hero."

I put the charm in my pocket. They were rare now, since there'd been a shortage a couple months ago when the Monster from our past had snapped them all up. Warlocks were busy making more, but the process wasn't easy and it took time.

"That'll at least give you a quick getaway," Cass said. "In case you need it."

"We might. Thanks." We'd need to go the slow way to get there, since a transportation charm would only work if you knew exactly where you were going. But it was always good to have a fast escape. I snagged a cup of coffee and practiced hefting a bag with one hand. I groaned. "Of course these folks valued rocks."

"I don't envy you climbing up to their settlement with rocks on your back."

I chuckled as I took the barstool next to her. "It'll be a workout."

"You sure you don't want me to come?"

I shook my head. "With the transport charm, we'll have a quick getaway in case we need it. That's my biggest concern. Otherwise, we're just trying to convince these people to give us a cure, since forcing them won't work. In that case, two people will do as well as three." I patted the backpack on the counter. "Especially if we have this."

"All right, then. But you've got your comms charm in case you need me. Give me your location, and I can be there in a flash."

I wrapped an arm around her and gave her a side hug. "You're the best."

"Nix would be here, too, if she didn't have to work."

"I know. Gotta keep the shop running."

"Exactly." Cass polished off her coffee, then stood. "And I have an appointment with a tomb in China. There's a sleeping charm there that is about to decay and explode."

"Better go save that tomb."

Cass saluted, then disappeared, using her transport powers.

Roarke entered the kitchen a second later. He grinned when he saw me, and heat curled in my belly. I could feel a blush rising, so I coughed and asked, "Your brother okay?"

"Still sedated. The guards are giving him constant doses." He frowned. "You're sure Connor knows his potions?"

"Yeah. If he said that's what to do, then you're safe."

"Good." Roarke pulled his thin black jacket off a post on the wall. "Ready to go?"

I finished my coffee and stood, then grabbed a granola bar from a bowl on the counter. "Ready now."

We arrived in Peru thirty minutes later, having taken the Underpath at Mad Mordecai's straight to a village called Cuzca in south-central Peru. I stepped out of the Underpass into the cool air, adjusting the heavy backpack full of rock. Roarke wore one, too, his a bit bigger than mine.

We were at the edge of a small, bustling village. Mountains rose high around us, and ominous clouds hovered overhead. Last night's research had revealed that it was the rainy season.

It was market day, with hundreds of people packed under the thatched roof stalls that sold colorful woven goods, toys, food, and tools. The chatter of voices was in a language I didn't recognize. Though the town was full of supernaturals—no humans allowed, just like Magic's Bend—I assumed they spoke Peruvian.

"How is this the Underpath exit?" I asked, examining the flat ground that we stood upon. There were no headstones. "Is it haunted?"

"No. There are mummies below."

"Mummies? My fave."

Roarke grinned, scanning the crowd of miscellaneous supernaturals. Peru was like the rest of the world in that it supported an assortment of our kind. And like the rest of the world, Peruvian supernaturals kept their distance from humans. Which meant that supernatural settlements like this were full of the weirdest looking supernaturals because they couldn't live in human cities.

"On your cue," Roarke said.

I shook my head. "Right. Sorry. Distracted. I've never seen a place like this. It's cool."

But I had a job to do. We knew that we could follow my dragon sense to the abandoned city of the Incate, but all the warnings in the treatises last night of booby traps made me want to ask a local for help. They always knew the most about their home turf and surrounding historical sites, so I wanted to make the best of that knowledge.

I called upon my dragon sense, asking it to take me to someone who would know the lay of the land and possibly how to find the Incate. It took a little while—lots of false starts—but finally it tugged me toward the market.

I pointed toward it. "That way."

We set off, joining the crush of bodies in the aisles between the stalls. Someone was cooking something that smelled divine, but there was also the smell of rain on the air and the scent of dried corn that filled huge woven stacks at the stall to my right.

Most of the people wore brightly colored ponchos woven in beautiful patterns. We threaded our way between the shoppers, heading toward the back of the market. The light was dimmer back here, and the market gave way to an alley.

I glanced at Roarke, who shrugged, then made my way into an alley. A darkened doorway to my left beckoned. It was open, so I entered.

The space was dimly lit but far more fabulously decorated than I would have anticipated. Woven wall hangings and rugs with beautiful wooden furniture abounded. An older man sat behind a heavy desk. He glanced up, his gray hair shining in the light of the Tiffany lamps.

He said something in a language I didn't recognize.

"Um, I'm sorry, I don't speak Peruvian," I said.

"English." His voice was deep and sonorous. Danger edged his words, a feeling more than anything. "That is fine. I speak English. I am Atilio. What do you need?"

"I am Del, and this is Roarke. We need to find the ancient city of the Incate and think you may be able to help."

He inclined his head. "I could, for a price."

I really hoped he didn't want my rocks. "What kind of price?"

"Ten thousand American, though I can only take you part of the way."

"We'll take it," Roarke said.

I gave Roarke a brief nod of agreement. Though I'd have loved for Atilio to take us all the way there, it would have been too good to be true. And I didn't want him witnessing what I did when we got there.

"Excellent." Atilio smiled and stood. "Cash first, then I will arrange the boat and the llamas."

"Boat and llamas?" I asked.

"Travel isn't easy in the Andes."

No, clearly not. And Atilio was like a Peruvian combination of The Godfather and a travel agent, apparently. I removed my backpack and pulled out a small leather pouch full of cash. It was a good thing Ancient Magic had been doing well lately, because these adventures were starting to get expensive.

I counted out the money and handed it off to Atilio. He counted it again, then whistled. A young man came from the back, smiled at us, then took the money.

Atilio waved his hand, indicating that we should follow. He led us out a larger exit onto a wide street, then down to the river. When we'd first arrived, I hadn't realized that there was a river here, but it made sense considering what we'd read last night. Wide rivers with some rapids cut through the valleys between the steep mountains all over this part of Peru.

The docks were bustling with people and boats. Atilio led us to a large one with a green and red hull. A rain shelter was built over the stern, and a short man stepped off to greet us. He wore the colorful knit hat that I'd noticed many of the men in town wearing.

"Del and Roarke, this is your captain, Diego. Once the llamas have arrived and have boarded, you will depart for Tarma."

"The llamas will get on the boat?" I asked. It didn't look like a very big boat—just one deck about twenty feet long.

"Yes." Atilio nodded.

Clomping footsteps sounded from behind me and I turned. The two biggest llamas I'd ever seen approached. They were easily ten feet tall, and each had fluffy white fur and a pair of curved horns. And fangs.

"Those are llamas?" I asked.

Atilio nodded. "Demon llamas. Blood drinkers."

"Oh." Never heard of those. I wasn't a fan of vampires—had never actually met one, since they were rare—but vampire llamas couldn't be so bad. I approached them both, holding out my hands for them to sniff. "Hey guys, how's—"

"Careful!" Atilio cried. "They bite!"

Though I heard him, I was more interested in the llamas. Like with Pond Flower and Ralph and Rufus, I could feel these animals. In a good way—like their souls communed with mine, or something hippy-dippy along those lines. They snuffled my hands.

"It's okay," Roarke murmured. "She has a way with animals."

The llamas bent their heads slightly and let me pet them. Their fur was slightly coarse and springy. I scratched them, keeping an eye on their fangs as I did so. They might like me, but I was still wary of four-inch fangs.

Killed by a llama was the last thing I wanted on my tombstone.

"Well, that will come in handy," Atilio said. "As you'll be riding them when you get off the boat."

I said goodbye to the llamas, and we boarded the boat. The llamas got on second, moving to the bow and sitting with their legs folded under them. They looked perfectly comfortable. Diego hurried around the boat, untying the lines to free us from the dock. He cranked the engine, and it roared softly.

"Diego will explain the rest of your journey." Atilio waved as we took off.

I waved back. "Thank you!"

Diego steered us away from the rest of the boats and down the river. The air was cooler on the water and the view of the mountains fantastic. They were steep and green, enormous sentries that I didn't look forward to climbing.

We motored on for about an hour, the llamas snoozing at the bow. Up ahead, the smooth expanse of water started to look choppy. Rocks?

"Hang on!" Diego shouted. "We're coming to some rapids!"

As we neared and I got a better view, my stomach dropped. Those weren't just some rapids. They were serious white water. And we were in this little wooden boat, not the sturdy rubber ones that I always saw on vacation leaflets for people who wanted to put on borrowed wetsuits and take a death ride down a river.

"I don't like this," I muttered.

"Don't worry!" Diego's cry was cheerful. "We're protected!"

As we bumped our way down the rapids, water spraying me in the face like an icy shower, I didn't feel that protected. With the ominous gray clouds overhead, the whole thing felt dire. But the llamas didn't appear to be concerned—they kept snoozing in the bow—and we never crashed on the rocks. After a while, I realized that I had a death grip on Roarke's arm, so I loosened it. Finally, the water smoothed out again.

"That's the worst of it," Diego said. "We're nearly there."

We'd reached an area where the mountains had opened up to reveal a floodplain. Diego pulled the boat over to the shore and walked around to the llamas.

"This is where I leave you," he said.

Thunder rumbled overhead.

Great.

Diego woke the llamas and led them off the boat onto the muddy bank, then turned to us. "You must ride the llamas across the floodplain to the mountains on the far side." He pointed to some steep mountains a couple miles away. They were verdant green, and the tops were ringed with dark gray clouds. "There is a village there. The llamas will know the way. Once you are there, they will take you to Pachato's son. He will recognize the llamas and know to help you."

"Thank you." Roarke gave me a boost onto the closest llama, who was warm and strong beneath me. There was no bridle, so I grabbed onto the fur of his neck. He didn't seem annoyed, fortunately.

Roarke climbed onto his llama. The beast was so big that even Roarke didn't look like he was too much weight.

"Anything else we should know?" Roarke asked.

"Yes." Diego scanned the floodplain behind us. "Do *not* get off the llama."

His tone sent a shiver across my skin. "Or what?"

"The reed monsters will rise. They recognize the llamas' footsteps and will let you pass unmolested. But if you were to walk upon the floodplain, they would awaken."

"Reed monsters?" I asked.

Diego nodded. "Impossible to kill. They are more magic than being. You'd be well served to stay on the llamas."

I patted my llama's neck and leaned down to whisper, "Don't ditch me, okay?"

We said goodbye to Diego and set off across the floodplain. The llamas knew the way, so I just hung on tight and watched the clouds overhead. They clustered and swirled, turning darker with every second.

"We're going to get a shower," Roarke said once we were halfway across and I could just barely make out the sight of rooftops in the distance.

A half second later, rain began to pour, a deluge that soaked me in an instant. Lightning lit up the day, so bright it was blinding. Thunder cracked, the loudest sound I'd ever heard. I almost screamed—and I wasn't normally much of a shrieker. My llama made a sound of pure terror, and bucked like a bull.

I tightened my grip on his fur, barely managing to hang on. But the lightning struck again, this time with louder thunder, and my llama bucked twice. I lost my grip and landed in the swampy grass. The llama bolted.

Crap! I jumped up.

"Del!" Somehow, Roarke managed to turn his llama. He reached down and pulled me up behind him.

But it was too late. The ground around us was shaking, vibrating with magic that made my skin prickle with awareness.

"Something big is coming," I said.

The ground burst to life, a humanoid figure made of reeds popping up from the earth. It was at least twenty feet tall and made all of grass, like some weird giant doll.

"Stay on the llama." Roarke's magic swirled around him, a dark cloud that smelled strongly of sandalwood and felt like a caress. I'd never been so close to him when he shifted.

He leaped off the llama before the transformation was complete. Probably to avoid knocking me off with his wings. By the time he hit the ground, he'd changed fully. His dark wings swept high. Fortunately, the backpack was still on his back, nestled between the roots of his wings, though his shirt had disappeared.

He took off into the sky, hurtling for the reed monster that lumbered toward us. I adopted my Phantom form, letting the icy magic flow through me. I was still gray-blue, but I blended better in the pouring gray rain.

I drew my sword from the ether as Roarke flew up to the reed monster's head. The creature had no eyes or nose or any other discernible feature.

"I need your help, buddy," I said to the llama. His head was swinging, but I didn't feel fear coming off him. Unlike his brother, this guy was brave. He wanted a fight. "Run at the monster's legs."

The llama snorted and took off. I held my sword out, aiming for the monster's left leg like some kind of weird medieval knight riding my demon llama into the joust.

As I reached the monster, I turned corporeal and slashed my sword through its leg, severing it. At the same time, Roarke gripped its head and tore it clean off. As my llama raced away, the monster crashed to its knees, splashing a thin wave of water up at me.

I glanced back over my shoulder.

The monster was rising!

Its leg had already started to grow back. So had its head. And in the distance, more monsters were popping out of the ground. In the sky, Roarke hovered like a dark angel of death. No matter how good I knew him to be, his demon form was always a little scary.

"We have to run for it!" I yelled.

"Go!" he yelled. "I'll follow."

My llama didn't need any convincing. It ran faster than a racehorse, hell-bent for leather—though I had no idea what that actually meant. Water splashed up from its pounding hoofs as rain poured from the sky. Roarke flew at my side, just above me. A quick glance behind revealed the reed monsters charging us. We had a lead of about fifty yards. I hoped we could keep it.

"Faster!" I cried at my llama.

Ahead, the other llama ran like its life depended on it. Which maybe it did. But we couldn't show up to Pachato's son without that llama. And I didn't want the poor thing to get lost.

"Get the llama!" I yelled at Roarke.

He turned his head toward me, indecision in his eyes.

"Leave me!" I screamed. "I'm fine!"

Roarke nodded sharply, then zoomed off, his wings carrying him twice as fast as my llama could run. I glanced behind me again, rain nearly blinding me, and prayed that I actually was going to be fine.

An ounce of relief flowed through me. The reed monsters were only about forty yards away. They were gaining, but our head start might save us. I turned back to the village, able to see the buildings through the rain.

Shit! What if I led these monsters straight into an innocent group of people?

Crap, crap, crap. Indecision warred. I could diverge, leading them away. As the llama jumped up onto a more solid part of ground, now out of the sloshy, reed-strewn floodplain, I turned around to check on the reed monsters.

They'd stopped dead in their tracks.

What?

The llama continued to gallop, faster than ever on this new, harder surface.

Understanding hit me. We'd left the reed monsters' territory when we'd gotten on the slightly higher, firmer ground. I glanced back again. The reed monsters were beginning to shrink, melting back into the ground.

Thank fates.

I turned to see Roarke riding his llama back toward me, wings closed behind him in what I assumed was supposed to be an aerodynamic stance.

"Are you okay?" he shouted through the rain.

"Yeah!" My llama galloped up to him, and he swung his around. Or, rather, his llama turned around to head toward town with us. There was no directing these beasts. They did exactly as they pleased. Which I respected.

Our animals slowed to a trot as we neared the village.

"You'd better shift back. Pachato's son will be a supernatural, but there could be humans here." Though what they would think of the demon llamas, I had no idea. But considering how threatening Roarke looked in his demon form...

It really wasn't the best first impression. Not if you wanted help, at least.

Roarke's magic swirled around him, and he returned to his human form. His shirt and jacket returned, dry because of his magic, but they were immediately soaked in the rain.

The llamas slowed their trot to a walk as we reached the buildings. There were only about thirty wooden structures, most glowing warmly with light. Though it was still midday, the rainclouds made it feel closer to dusk.

The cobblestone street ran with water, and the llamas' hooves clacked against it. Slightly ahead on the left, a curtain in a window flicked open, revealing a shadowed face. A moment later, the door swung open.

"Ilyapa! Maita!" a man called.

The llamas swung toward the voice, then trotted over.

"Must be Pachato's son," I said.

Roarke nodded.

The man stepped out into the rain and scratched both llamas behind the ears. "My father must have sent you. I am Sandro."

He spoke English. I didn't look very local, probably.

"Hello, Sandro," I said. "I am Del, and this is Roarke. Your father did send us. We need help reaching the ancient city of the Incate."

He glanced up at the ominous clouds. "In this weather?"

I shrugged. "We can wait a while to see if it passes."

He nodded eagerly. "Yes, yes. It will pass. Come in. Get warm and dry."

We climbed off the llamas as a young boy came out, his face lighting when he saw the massive creatures.

"Ilyapa! Maita!" he cried.

The llamas bent low so he could scratch their ears. Sandro said something in Peruvian, and the boy led the llamas around the house.

"Come, come." He gestured us inside.

We followed him into the warm, dimly lit space. It was simple but pretty, with wooden furniture and a colorful woven covering on the couch. Before we could step too far inside, Sandro turned and stopped us, holding out his hands. "First, your clothes."

"Oh, sorry!" We were dripping all over his floor.

"Not a problem." He held his hands closer to us, and a strong warm wind rushed over us. A bit like a giant hand dryer in an airport bathroom.

Within seconds, my front half was dry. It was freaking delightful. So I turned and let him dry my back half. When we were fully dry, he stepped back and turned off his wind power.

"Thank you for your hospitality," Roarke said.

"Don't thank me until you have had a drink." Sandro turned toward the simple kitchen and puttered around.

I glanced at Roarke, who shrugged, then nodded toward the small table surrounded by four chairs. We sat. Roarke was about a foot and a half taller than Sandro—he'd had to duck coming in—and I had to suppress a giggle at the sight of him slowly lowering himself into the tiny chair.

When it didn't crack under his weight, relief was clear on his face.

Sandro carried over two cups that were topped with thick foam. He handed us each one. "Chicha de Jora. A local beer."

"Thank you." I took it and sipped through the foam. Sweet at first, and then sour, it wasn't like any beer I'd ever had. "Delicious."

I meant it, too. Though it was a bit odd and the foam tickled my nose, it was tasty.

Sandro got a glass for himself, then sat. "Tell me what I can do for you."

We explained about our need to reach the ancient city of the Incate.

"I can take you partway there. Then, it is up to you." He frowned, worry creasing his brow. "Though you may not like what you find."

CHAPTER SEVEN

After a meal of Causa, a Peruvian potato and avocado casserole, we departed Sandro's house once the rain had stopped. The sun peeked out from behind the clouds, turning the cool day warm. Sandro led us out of the village and toward a path that wound its way up the mountain. Since his town butted right up to the base of the green slope, it was an immediate incline.

The path was steep and rough. Within minutes, I was panting hard, in part because of the bag of rocks on my back. *Of course* the Incate valued rocks. Who would want to carry them up this slope? After a journey like this, they had to be worth a lot.

Roarke tried to take my pack from me, probably because I was panting like a dog after a long run, but I shrugged him off.

"I've got it."

"Don't be stubborn. You'll need to be able to use your arms."

I almost growled at him, but bit it back. No need to be a brat. "Thanks. But really, I want to carry my own weight."

And in fairness, my pack was sized for me. His was a lot bigger.

He reached out and squeezed my hand. I squeezed back.

We'd been hiking for several hours when Sandro suddenly stopped. I pulled to a halt abruptly. Ahead of us, the path widened. And suddenly, it was paved in strange, shaped stones.

Sandro turned, his voice serious. "You must put your feet exactly where I put my feet."

We nodded. I was familiar with this kind of trap. No way I'd be going rogue, not if we had an inside man leading the way.

Sandro began to walk across the stones, slowly and steadily. The path seemed totally random. But I followed, muscles straining as I took wide steps, careful not to tread on the wrong rock.

We were nearly to the end when a rabbit darted out of the bushes, landing on the rocks and then bounding away. My heart leaped into my throat, and sweat broke out on my skin.

Oh fates—would its weight set off the trap?

But nothing happened. I'd almost relaxed when a louder rustling sounded from behind it.

"Incoming," Roarke said.

A puma lunged out of the forest to my left, its big paws hitting the rocks as it chased the rabbit across the path. The cat was so fast that it was never at risk of the booby trap. It'd bounded off into the forest by the time the ground beneath my feet began to rumble.

Sandro stepped off the path, having reached the end.

"Hurry!" he cried as the ground beneath me rose up, rock cracking and breaking.

I lost my footing, crashing to my butt against the rock as it grew around me.

Like a giant mouth, rising out of the ground to swallow me whole.

The path had morphed into a huge, fanged maw that would swallow wayward walkers. I was alone inside the crevasse of rock, and I scrambled to my feet. There was no way I could climb out, so I adopted my Phantom form. I'd completely lost my orientation. If I walked through the stone the wrong way, I could end up *in* the mountain.

I swallowed hard. As I was about to pick a random direction, a shadow above blocked out the light. I glanced up.

"Roarke!"

He swept down, wings carrying him low enough to grab my outstretched hand. He pulled me free of the now-closing pit, and I thanked fate that he was one of the rare few who could touch a Phantom. My heart thundered as he gathered me close and flew to the other side of the path.

Sandro watched us, his jaw open. "You are not normal."

Roarke put me on the ground. "What's normal among supernaturals, anyway?"

Sandro inclined his head. "Fair point."

He tilted his head to watch the path become flat again. I turned as well, watching the stone settle back into a flat path. Had I still been trapped in the great mouth of enchanted stone, I'd have been swallowed into the ground with no one the wiser. How many bodies were under there? I shuddered.

"I told you to walk where I walked," Sandro said.

I grinned. "You weren't joking."

"Come." He turned, heading back down the path.

We continued to climb, hiking higher into the mountains. Three times, Sandro stopped us so he could throw a large rock onto the path ahead. Every time he did, the pressure of the stone hitting the path ignited a giant rockfall. The boulders tumbled down in a roar.

"I'm glad you're our guide," I said as I watched the deadly scene. The rocks came so fast they would have caught us for sure.

"You must have paid my father well."

I shrugged.

Soon after, we reached a break in the path. The ground had long ago fallen away. Forty feet across, the path resumed.

"Here is where I leave you." Sandro pointed across the crevasse. "You must get across. Then continue to climb. From there, you will find the settlement. Look carefully. It is covered by plants."

"Thank you, Sandro," Roarke said.

Sandro inclined his head. "My pleasure. Good luck."

"We're going to need it, I think." I couldn't look away from the massive gap in the mountain that we were supposed to cross.

Sandro left, ambling back down the mountain.

"I can fly us across."

"Okay. But give me a sec. I want to know if there was once a bridge here." And it would give me a good opportunity to practice my magic before the big show at the Incate settlement when I had to bring the healer back from the past so we could get a cure.

I drew in a deep breath and let the magic flow through me. I sent my magic toward the empty space where a bridge might have been. The familiar blue glow spread out from me, racing across the ground. As it traveled, a spindly rope bridge appeared.

Just like in that Indiana Jones movie. I swallowed hard, remembering what had happened to that bridge.

"Yeah, I'll definitely take that ride, thanks," I said.

Roarke laughed. "I can't blame you. That would not pass any kind of safety test."

"No." I let my magic fade, willing the bridge to disappear back to the past from which I'd called it. The process was slow because the bridge was quite long.

I had a theory that the larger the space I brought back from the past, the longer it took to appear or disappear. As if my magic had to fill the space or drain away from it, and that took time.

"Let's go." I nodded at Roarke.

In a swirl of magic, he shifted to his demon form and swept me up in the air. I clung to him, grateful for the ride.

"I can't look down." I squeezed my eyes tight as he flew us across the open space that plunged to the river below, thousands of feet below.

Roarke chuckled.

When we landed, I drew in a breath. "I'm not normally afraid of heights, but that was a bit much, even for me."

"You had that Indiana Jones scene in your head, didn't you?"

"How did you know?"

"Hard not to think of it." He smiled. "Ready to keep going?"

I tilted my head back to examine the path that led up the steep mountainside. The trek was getting serious, now. "Can't wait."

We hiked, Roarke insisting on taking the lead, keeping our eyes and ears alert for any booby traps or danger. The air grew mistier and colder the higher we climbed, until we were within the clouds themselves.

"A cloud forest," I said, wonder filling me. "I read about them last night. We're actually in the clouds."

"Incredible."

"Really is." My crazy life and the trials it was bringing lately had also brought me to some amazing places, at least.

Then we hiked higher than the clouds, ascending nearly to the top of the green mountain. Around us, other mountains popped up above the clouds.

"I feel like I'm on top of the world." I grinned.

"We are. And I think we're here."

"Yeah." Upon closer inspection, the mountaintop—which still extended up another few hundred yards ahead of us—wasn't just naturally bumpy. Foliage grew over tumbled-down buildings, the land reclaiming the space for itself. "Sandro wasn't kidding when he said this place was covered in plants."

Here and there, stone walls peeked out, but they were well hidden.

"Shall we search for the healer's building?" Roarke asked.

"Yes." We'd decided that we would go straight to the healer before I brought the place back from the past, then pretend to be traders looking for a cure to the curse. I wanted to spend as little time as possible interacting with people from the past, because who knew what they'd do to us?

I called upon my dragon sense, asking it to take me to the building where the healer had once lived. It took a while, but eventually it caught on, tugging me toward the top of the mountain.

We hiked up the mountainside, finding an abandoned set of stairs that was distinguishable only by its slope. Tumbled-down buildings crouched on either side, but our path was relatively easy—though it did make me pant like a dog at the beach.

"All the way up?" Roarke asked.

"Yep. The elite usually lived at the top of the mountain in settlements like this, so it makes sense the healer would be up there, too. Gotta tend to the king's every boo-boo!"

"It's good to be king."

I panted a laugh and kept climbing. We passed a big, open flat space that had probably once been some kind of courtyard, then continued to climb. There were larger buildings at the top, all of them tumbled down and roofless like the ones below.

But it was a smaller building that my dragon sense pulled me toward.

"That one." I pointed, then led Roarke toward it. There was an alley to the right, a narrow space between two broken-down half walls. "Let's get in the alley for a little cover."

"Good idea."

We squeezed in between the two buildings, which wasn't bad because the walls only came up to our thighs. I dug into the small pocket on my backpack and pulled out the two potions from Connor. They were neon orange, and I'd bet big money they didn't taste like orange soda.

I handed one off to Roarke. "Drink this. It'll allow us to communicate with the healer."

"Excellent. My Incate is terrible." He unscrewed the cap on the little vial and tossed it back, grimacing.

I followed, almost gagging at the foul taste of bitter medicine. I'd found that the prettier Connor's potions, the grosser they usually tasted.

I coughed. "Sure hope that worked."

"Me too."

"Ready?"

Roarke nodded. I let my power fill me, calling upon my ability to bring back the past. I'd decided to go back to about 1050 AD, hoping that it would do the trick. Magic flowed through my limbs, then spread out from me, glowing and blue.

First, the plants receded, revealing the walls that they had tried to consume. Then the stone walls on either side of us grew up quickly, their roofs appearing seconds later. They blocked out the sun, casting shadow over our hiding place.

Through the gap in the alley, I could see out to the street. Other buildings grew up across from us, one story high and constructed of perfectly carved stones. No mortar for the Incate, not with masons like that.

"I think you're good," Roarke murmured.

"Yeah." I'd definitely brought back the healer's house, so I pulled back on my magic. I couldn't tell how much of the Incate settlement I had brought back from the past. Maybe all of it. When we were through here, I'd have to be careful to send it all back to its proper time period.

Quietly, I shifted toward the alley entrance, peeking out. The first person I saw was walking away from us down the street. And he was blue. A Phantom.

If they were like me, as Mordaca had said, they could also be in human form. But that one chose Phantom. Across the street, a blue shadow flashed by a window. Another Phantom.

Though I would clearly blend in with the crowd better if I was in Phantom form, I decided not to shift or it'd reveal my cursed state.

When I was certain they weren't looking out the window and that no one was on the little street, I hurried out and turned right, seeking the door of the healer's house.

I knocked briefly on the wood, then pushed it open and stepped inside, Roarke behind me. It was a bit rude, but I'd risk it so as not to be seen.

The space was small, with a fire burning sluggishly in the hearth on the left side of the room. A smiling woman looked up from behind a wooden table. This was clearly a shop, with shelves of vials and potions behind her. Thank fates. At least she was expecting people to just show up, and I didn't walk in on her naked.

Her smile faltered slightly. "You are not from here?"

There was a slight lag on my understanding of her words. The potion. "No. We are traders from across the sea. We seek your help."

After a moment, she nodded. She, too, seemed to experience a slight lag in understanding my words. "What do you need?"

From behind her, a head peeked out of a doorway leading to a back room. Eyes met mine before the head disappeared behind the wall. Nerves prickled my skin.

I met the healer's gaze. "A friend of ours has been cursed with a spell that we believe originated here. It makes him susceptible to suggestion and mind control. Do you happen to have a cure?"

A thoughtful gleam entered her eyes. She hesitated, clearly thinking. "Yes. That is possible. And I do have a cure, but only for the right price."

From behind her, the head popped out again. I thought I might've heard whispers, but I couldn't quite tell. My skin prickled with unease.

"We've brought obsidian." Roarke removed his pack and took it to her table, unzipping it.

The first thing she did was study the zipper and the nylon, taking ages.

Hurry up! We needed to get out of here. I didn't like the whispering people in the other room.

"You could have the bag as well," I said.

She didn't respond, just reached into the bag and withdrew a piece of red obsidian. Her eyes brightened. "This is very rare. Only the emperor has red obsidian." She reached in and withdrew the green. "And this!"

Well, at least we'd gotten the right trade goods. If I could kiss my books, I would have.

"Is this enough for the cure?" Roarke asked.

"Yes." Her gaze snapped to me. To my shoulders, actually, where the straps of my bag cut in. "Does she have a bag of the obsidian also?"

"Yes." I took it off and put it on her table. "We would like to cure our friend quickly"—and get the hell out of here—"so if you could make two doses, I would be happy to give you this bag of obsidian as well."

She nodded resolutely. "Yes. Yes. It will only take a moment to mix it."

Fates, I hoped this really was the cure. But there was no way to tell until we actually took it.

She set about gathering vials and a mortar and pestle. I looked at the back room. It was silent now, but it didn't make me feel any better. Tension hung in the air.

As she was pouring a liquid into a vial, I asked her, "Do we just drink it?"

"Yes. If the cursed is not a Phantom, they need only drink it. The curse does not cling as strongly to the non-Phantom."

"And if they are part Phantom?"

"Then the cursed must drink the potion and kill the one who cursed them."

Oh fates. Did that mean I had to kill Roarke's brother?

There was rustling in the room beyond, making my hair stand on end. "Is the potion complete?"

The healer put two wooden stoppers into the vials and held them out. "Yes. Finished."

Roarke took them, tucking them into the pocket of his jacket. As soon as he had them, I reached for the transport charm in my pocket. If we could just get out of here, this place would disappear back into the past without my magic to sustain it.

Before I could withdraw the stone, however, men surged from the back room, hurling potion bombs at us. They were all in Phantom form, their blue glow lighting up the dimly lit room.

"What are you doing?" the healer cried.

I dodged the bombs, but there were too many. One hit me in the stomach and exploded in a poof of gray powder, immediately making me woozy and weak.

"They are traders! Do not harm them, idiot!" the healer cried.

Beside me, Roarke was hit with two potion bombs. I stumbled to my knees, my head swimming. There were six assailants. Four of them went to Roarke, hitting him with three more potion bombs. *Probably because he's so big,* I thought hazily.

"What is the meaning of this, husband?" the healer demanded.

I blinked, trying to clear my double vision, but it did no good. At least I wasn't passing out. A man came to me and bound my wrists in a heavy rope.

"They are foreign," the tallest man said. "Too strange. We must bring them to the emperor."

The healer looked at the piles of obsidian on the table, clearly loath to bring any of this to the attention of the emperor and possibly lose her payment.

"We will be rewarded, wife," the man said.

"They are just traders." She gestured to us. "Let them go."

"No, they are more than that. I can feel it. We must take them to the emperor."

Dread curled in my stomach. Before I could protest—though I wasn't sure I was even capable—two of the men dragged me up by my arms and hauled me out of the house.

I needed to send this place back to the past.

Through my hazy thoughts, it took everything I had to call upon my magic. I'd have to retract it all, drawing it back into me and sending them back to the eleventh century where they belonged.

But nothing happened.

Panic beat frantic wings inside my chest.

The man dragging me through the street shook me. "Do not try to use your foreign magic. It will not work. The potion prevents it."

Did he mean the sedative that was making me so woozy? He must, because my magic was doing no good. Sweat broke out on my skin.

The past was here to stay.

And I was stuck in it.

CHAPTER EIGHT

They dragged us through the street, past magnificent stone buildings and up a staircase bordered on one side by an incredible fountain that flowed all the way down to the lower level.

Roarke was so heavily sedated that the men had to half drag, half carry him. By the time we reached the very top of the mountain, they were all panting with exhaustion.

Ahead of us was a huge building with the front wall entirely missing. It probably commanded a great view of the city and mountains beyond, but I was too drugged out of my mind to even turn my head.

In the middle of the building was a huge stone throne. A Phantom man sat upon it. Though his entire form glowed blue, I had to assume that the headdress he wore was made of gold. He looked like the type to deck himself out in gold. Attendants stood on either side.

"What have you brought me?" His voice was so deep and loud that I imagined it echoing through the mountains.

"Strangers, emperor." The man holding me shook me by the arm. "They appeared in my house."

My head bobbled on my neck, feeling like it might fall off. Whatever they'd put in those potion bombs, it was strong stuff.

The emperor waved an elegant hand at us. "Check them."

One of his attendants hurried forward. The Phantom's magic smelled of a fresh breeze, but the coldness in his eyes made me shiver. He got too close to me, sniffing deeply, then squeezing my arm. His touch felt like ice. He then went to Roarke, repeating the procedure.

Finally, he turned to the emperor. "A World Walker and a demon hybrid. Dangerous beings."

"What do you suggest we do with them?" the emperor asked.

Send us on our way. Kick us out of the city.

"Use them in the sacrifice," the healer said. "The gods will be pleased at their strength, and they will no longer be a problem for us."

Use us in the sacrifice?

I'd read that the Incate had practiced human sacrifice, just like their human counterparts, the Inca, but this was too much.

I opened my mouth to protest, but the best I could do was rasp out a weak, "No."

This sedative was so damned strong!

The emperor nodded. "It is fated that they would arrive on the day of the great sacrifice. Send them to the Itatoapia. We will begin at sundown, as planned."

Holy fates, my power was now biting me in the ass. My magic was great and all, but it sure had a dark side.

The men dragged us from the room. I did everything I could to kick and fight, but it was like moving through pudding.

They pulled us out into the courtyard, and the emperor's attendant approached. "Put them in the holding chamber. I will gather the chains, then we will go to the Itatoapia."

Chains? My head was spinning as they half carried me across the courtyard and tossed us in a small stone room. When the wooden door slammed shut, the room turned black as pitch.

We were in a holding cell.

Where we waited to be sacrificed to the gods.

"Del?" Roarke slurred.

Shit, shit, shit. We were screwed. I could barely move, my power was kaput, and Roarke was in no better shape. Also, it was nearly sunset. The sun had been low in the sky just a moment ago. We were weak as kittens and about the be *sacrificed.*

Think, think, think.

My bound hands trembled as I reached for my left jacket pocket, seeking the transport charm. I fumbled until I found it, drawing it out of my pocket.

"Roarke," I slurred. "I'm going to throw this. Roll into the dust when it blasts up."

"Ooh-kay."

I chucked the stone against the ground, but nothing happened.

"Damn it." Normally, a cloud of silvery dust would poof up, and we'd step into it, transported to wherever we desired.

But the holding cell had magic that blocked escape. Which was no surprise, really. I scooted forward, woozy, and grabbed the stone, then shoved it back into my pocket.

I *really* wished I'd made a point of stealing more demon powers. I might have had something in my arsenal—like a resistance to potions—that could have helped. But I hadn't. And we were trapped. Powerless. We couldn't fight, but that didn't mean my friends couldn't. If only they could reach us. I dug into my pocket, seeking my cell phone. I fumbled it out and pressed the little button. It glowed to life, bright and welcoming.

As expected, I had no signal up here.

But GPS… Since I'd brought the past to the present instead of vice versa, that meant the satellites were still hanging up there in outer space, observing an ancient ritual down here on Earth that they'd never before witnessed.

I fumbled with the buttons, my fingers moving so slowly. Eventually, our GPS coordinates were revealed. Carefully, I laid the phone on the ground so I could see the numbers, then raised my hands and pressed my fingertips to the charm around my neck.

"Cass?" I slurred.

"Del!" she cried.

"Shhhh." I didn't want to alert the guards, if there were any. Not like we could get out of here on our own steam. I did my best to mutter out our coordinates, repeating them once I had finished.

"I'm—"

The door to the cell slammed open, cutting off Cass's words.

"What is that?" the guard demanded. He stomped over and grabbed the cell phone, muttering to himself.

I sagged back against the wall, praying that Cass had gotten the message about where we were.

"Black magic," the guard muttered. "Trespassers. Food for the gods."

Food for the gods? I was food for nobody.

Annoyed, I spat at him.

He backhanded me across the face. Unfortunately, he was a beast of a Phantom, and the blow knocked me clean out.

When I came to, I saw the sky. It glowed in hues of yellow, orange, pink, and purple.

What a beautiful sunset.

Then I heard the voice chanting overhead. And felt the chains at my wrists and ankles, the hard rock beneath my back.

Holy fates, I was chained to a rock about to be sacrificed.

My heart leaped into my throat. I jerked against my bindings, my muscles finally responding to my demands, at least a little bit. The sedative had worn off partially, but I was still weak.

I thrashed my head, trying to see around me.

Roarke lay next to me, chained to his own rock. He still wore his black jacket and jeans, and I was clothed, too. Thank fates for small favors. We were surrounded on all sides by a crowd of eager Phantom faces.

At my head, the emperor's main attendant stood, a glinting blade in his hand.

A scream built in my throat. I swallowed it. I wouldn't give these assholes the satisfaction. And if they were hoping to sacrifice a virgin, they'd be sorely disappointed. I sure as hell wasn't going to start screaming my head off.

The attendant was chanting in tune with another Phantom who stood over Roarke. I could no longer make out what they were saying, so Connor's translation potion must have worn off.

The sun was dipping in the sky. If I lifted my head, I could just make it out as it began to sink behind the peaks in the distance.

But something was flying toward us, silhouetted by the sinking sun.

Hope rose in my chest, a light that couldn't be extinguished. Closer and closer, the beast flew. Finally, golden feathers glinted in the light.

Aidan, flying in his griffin form!

Cass and Nix rode upon his back. When they were close enough that I could see their eyes, Cass leaned over and shot fire from her fingertips, blasting the Phantoms.

Though I didn't think it could harm them, it sure did startle them. The crowd jumped back, gasping. The two attendants who were chanting and holding daggers stopped abruptly.

"Hang on!" Cass cried.

I wanted to whoop with joy, but we weren't saved yet. Only a Phantom could harm another Phantom. Or Roarke. But both of us were a bit incapacitated.

Cass and Nix were no dummies, though. They didn't try to wage a war they couldn't win. Instead, Aidan dropped them off at our altars, then flew in a tight circle around us, roaring like a lion on steroids and thrashing his claws. As far as I could tell, he was just trying to scare the Phantoms away, which wasn't a bad plan. He was pretty freaking scary.

I called upon my metal magic, praying that the sedative had worn off enough that my magic could flow through. It was weak at first, but it began to surge within me.

While I worked, Cass used her Mirror Mage powers to mimic the power of those around her and turned herself into a Phantom. She glowed blue and bright, but if she wanted to fight them, she'd need a weapon.

As if on cue, Nix conjured a sword and tossed it to Cass, who caught it and turned on the attendants.

"You think you're going to sacrifice my *deirfiúr*?" she screamed, lunging toward them.

I fed my magic into my chains as Nix conjured a massive pair of bolt cutters. I was slow, the sedative still in my system, but it finally melted off me as Nix cut the last of the chains binding Roarke.

I staggered to my feet, woozy from the potion.

Aidan was still flying circles, and Cass was swinging her sword like a warrior on speed. I wanted to join her, lunging for the nearest Phantom and stealing his power for my own. Not just for the strength or for vengeance, but to prove that I had some say in my fate. That I was in control.

But I was too weak from the potion, and Cass's elegant movement caught my eye. She wasn't trying to kill anyone. Wounds were limited to legs and arms. Of course. In my drugged stupor, I'd forgotten the most important rule.

Don't change history.

Killing someone would definitely change history.

I pulled back on my desire to wreak havoc and steal powers.

"We're good to go!" Nix cried as she pulled Roarke up.

He was looking more alert than he had, but he still wasn't at full strength. They'd loaded him up with the magical equivalent of elephant tranquilizers. I hurried to him.

Aidan landed next to me, thudding heavily on the ground between the two altars. Cass raced back to us, keeping her sword at the ready.

"Del, you take Roarke!" Cass cried. "I'll take Aidan and Nix!"

The Phantoms began to close in. Didn't want to lose their sacrifices, the jerks.

I dug into my pocket, pulling out the black transportation stone that Cass had given me, then grabbed Roarke's hand. As Cass disappeared with Aidan and Nix, I hurled the stone to the ground. Silver dust poofed up, and I lunged into it, dragging Roarke.

I envisioned Ancient Magic, my true home, and the ether sucked me toward our shop in a flash. We hadn't agreed on a place to meet, but whenever I thought of home, this was it.

When we stumbled out into the shop, I saw Cass, Nix, and Aidan, now in his human form with a broken vase next to him.

My knees weakened. We'd made it. Roarke stumbled, but managed to stay upright.

I panted. "Oh fates, you made it just in time."

Cass grinned, but it had a slightly sick look to it. She raised a shaky hand to her hair and pushed it through the sleek red strands. "Yeah. That guy had a knife held right over you."

It glinted in my memory, turning my stomach. I stumbled over to Cass and Nix, who hugged me tightly. "Thanks, guys."

"Anytime." Nix squeezed me tight.

"Good thinking with the coordinates," Cass said. "Though it took us a little while to figure it out."

I started shaking, the stress hitting me a bit late. Being chained to a sacrificial altar could really screw a girl up.

"I've got it." Roarke's voice slurred from behind me.

I turned to see him holding up two vials. The cure.

He'd gotten the cure.

Then he swayed.

"Whoa, buddy." Aidan hurried over, catching him and grabbing the two vials. He wrapped an arm around Roarke's waist, supporting him. "What'd they give you?"

"Some kind of sedative." My muscles still felt wobbly. "They really dosed him, though. Five times as much as I got."

"Because he's such a big bastard," Aidan said. "If I wanted to sacrifice him, I'd do the same."

"Let's get you guys to Connor," Nix said. "Maybe he has something to flush this out of your system."

We staggered down to P & P, Nix running ahead to let Connor know that we were coming. I leaned heavily on Cass while Roarke leaned on Aidan. We were definitely steadier on our feet, but still a disaster. By the time we made it to P & P, Nix had pulled a couple chairs a bit closer to the door.

I collapsed into one next to Roarke and met her gaze. "You're the best."

"And you're drunk." She grinned. "Not on liquor, which is too bad, but on whatever was in that potion."

"Drunk is right." She'd hit the nail on the head. That was exactly what this felt like. A serious bender. I just hoped there wasn't a hangover.

Though there were a few other patrons bent over a scrabble board, they were uninterested in our antics. In fairness, we did just look like two folks who'd had too good a Tuesday afternoon.

Connor hurried out of the back, an assortment of vials clutched in his hand. He was wearing another band T-shirt today. The words swam, but eventually I made out the name Technicolor Monkeys.

"Oh, you guys look rough." He set his vials on the little table near Roarke and bent to peer into the big guy's eyes. "Yeah, you're stoned out of your mind, all right. A couple more doses and you'd be dead."

"You know what it is?" I asked.

Connor nodded and pointed to Roarke's eyes. "There's a telltale blue ring there. A side effect of the Rowdensus Potion. It's pretty ancient —kinda like pot and alcohol mixed together, but in a really strong dose. Enough to make you woozy, weak, and give you double vision."

Yep, those were the symptoms.

"Can you get it out of their system?" Nix demanded.

"Yep. Though they'll feel like shit."

"A hangover." I didn't phrase it as a question.

"Exactly."

"Might as well get to it, then." I grimaced at the thought. I *hated* hangovers. It was the reason I filled my coffee mug only half full of wine. Slopping around with a headache and sour stomach was the last way I ever wanted to spend the day.

Connor passed me a vial and helped Roarke drink a larger one that he held up to his lips. Unfortunately, the stuff was a glimmering pink color, so pretty that it had to be disgusting.

I uncorked it, sucked in a deep breath, then downed the thing.

I was pleasantly delighted at the taste of fresh strawberry.

That was, until the potion kicked in, flushing the last of the poison from my system. I started sweating immediately, soaking through the back of my shirt and turning my hair damp.

Across from me, Roarke's brow gleamed in the warm light.

Then the hangover hit. A giant pounded on drums inside my head while my stomach turned sour as month-old milk.

"Oh, I'm going to die." I collapsed back against the chair.

"Looks like it worked!" Connor's voice was way too cheerful.

"Now you definitely look like you were drunk," Nix said.

I leaned over so I could see my reflection in one of the decorative mirrors on the wall.

Sallow skin, bags under my eyes, hair limp as spaghetti. Yep. Drunk as a skunk and now sober as a nun.

Perfect.

I drew in a shuddery breath. "Could I have a coffee and some water? Possibly an entire bottle of aspirin?"

"On it." Connor hurried off, stopping briefly to turn down the music that pumped over the speakers.

My head immediately felt ten percent better. Connor was a hero.

Roarke's hand closed around mine. I glanced up to meet his eyes. "Thanks for getting us out of there."

"Thank Cass." I grinned up at her. "She got the message right in time."

Cass pulled up a spindly wooden chair and plopped into it. "Thank magic. That was some sticky stuff you were in."

"No kidding."

"But worth it." Roarke gestured to the two vials that Aidan now held.

"If that works on your brother, you're going to need a truth teller," Aidan said.

"Good thought," Roarke said. "I don't know how to read him anymore."

"Isn't Alton, from the FireSouls, a truth teller?" Nix asked.

"Yes!" I'd forgotten about him. He was one of the ten warriors who lived at the FireSoul complex with Corin and Flora.

"Want me to go see if I can get him?" Cass asked.

"Yes, thank you," Roarke said. "You could bring him to my place."

She stood and saluted. "Will do."

Aidan followed her out, and Nix headed to the bar to get a drink.

I took one of the vials from the table by Roarke and downed it, then leaned toward him and whispered, "I won't kill your brother."

Understanding glinted in his eyes. There was every chance that I could only be free of this curse if I killed Caden, who'd given it to me. And if that were true, then the Shadows might actually accomplish their awful plan.

"Don't think about it." He leaned over and pressed a kiss to my lips. "We will figure it out."

Though I hoped he was right, it was hard to believe it.

CHAPTER NINE

After quick showers at my place, we arrived at Roarke's as the sun was setting. All this time zone hopping meant that I kept repeating sunsets. I hadn't wanted another viewing of this one, but at least the circumstances were better.

I might've had the worst hangover in the history of time, but that was better than being chained to a rock waiting to be sacrificed.

Roarke and I hadn't talked any more about curing me of the curse. By unspoken agreement, we'd deal with his brother first and see what we could learn. Anyway, it'd taken ten years for the curse to decay on Caden. I had time.

We climbed the porch stairs to Roarke's place just as Cass's voice sounded.

"Hey, guys!" she shouted from behind.

I turned to look into the woods. She and Alton stood about fifty yards from the house, deep in the shadows of the trees. Smart not to transport too close—protection charms usually didn't like that kind of thing.

They approached, coming out of the gloom. Alton hadn't changed since I'd last seen him at the FireSoul headquarters. He was a handsome black man, almost as tall as Roarke, with hard eyes, a strong jaw, and a dashing scar across his cheek. He wore burnished red leather armor, and though I favored black, it ignited a slight tinge of envy.

Maybe I should mix it up some.

Alton and Cass climbed the stairs to the porch.

"Good to see you, Del." He nodded at me, then stuck his hand out toward Roarke. "I'm Alton."

Roarke gripped it and shook. "Roarke. Good to meet you, and thank you for coming."

Alton nodded to Cass and me. "The Triumvirate are prophesied to do great things. The League of FireSouls is dedicated to helping them."

"Thank you," I said. The League had come to our aid months ago when Cass had faced off against the Monster.

Alton nodded, then we followed Roarke into the house. Cass, Alton, and I went into the living room while Roarke went to the basement to fetch Caden.

He returned a few minutes later. The demons carried Caden's chair, to which he was still chained and unconscious. Connor's new, stronger potion had put Caden's body into stasis, which had been super helpful considering that the stasis negated any need for bodily function. The last thing we'd wanted to do was have to repeatedly unchain a guy as strong as Caden.

The demons set him down in the middle of the living room. Cass and Alton positioned themselves behind Caden, while I waited. Roarke drew a vial out of his pocket and approached, tilting Caden's head back and pouring the liquid down his throat. It took some coaxing, but he got Caden to swallow the stuff.

Unable to bear the suspense, I approached and leaned in, sniffing near Caden's head.

Relief coursed through me, weakening my muscles. "He no longer smells."

"Good." Roarke went to the kitchen, then returned a moment later with another small vial. He held it up. "This should wake him up."

It was an antidote to the sedative, also brewed by Connor. Roarke poured it down Caden's throat.

Immediately, Caden sputtered awake, shaking his head.

"What—Where am I?" His wide eyes darted around the room. They were a paler gray than Roarke's, but familiar.

Suddenly, he looked so much younger, and smaller, than Roarke. My heart twisted in my chest. This man was Roarke's *brother*. And the Shadows had stolen him.

"You're safe, brother," Roarke said.

Caden's head whipped toward the voice. "Roarke!"

"Caden."

"Cade," his brother corrected.

Roarke nodded, something strange passing across his face. Like he'd once called him that but had stopped since their estrangement. A small smile tugged at the corners of his lips. "Cade. What do you remember?"

Cade blinked, his expression clearing. As if his memory were coming back. Fortunately, I spotted no cunning on his face, and Alton would be able to confirm it.

"Everything." Devastation laced Caden's voice. "All of it. And all of it terrible."

I glanced at Alton, who nodded. *Truth.*

"But you cured me?" Cade asked. "I no longer feel the Shadows' presence."

"Yes, we found the cure."

Cade sagged, relief evident on his face. Then he straightened, his gaze darting to Roarke. "Everything I've done... It's all terrible."

"I know." Pain crossed Roarke's face. "But you weren't in control."

"No." Grief laced his voice. "But I sought out the Shadows. I asked them to make me stronger—to give me more power. You had so much, Roarke. I just wanted to be equal."

"And they helped you," Roarke said. "You have several new powers. You used those powers to escape the Order prison."

"Yes. But at a cost."

"So it was mutual?" I asked. "A partnership?"

"At first. When I was young and dumb."

I could relate to young and dumb. I'd been young and plenty dumb. Was arguably still a bit of both.

"Why did they curse you?" Roarke asked. "They are powerful. Surely they can do their own bidding."

"They cannot walk upon the earth. At least, not far from the small portals they create. They are bound by hell's magic. But their plans mean they have work to do on Earth. They have to communicate with the demons who are on this side."

"That's what you did," I said.

"Yes. Because I'm half demon, I can walk between Earth and the Underworld." Cade licked his lips, and I suddenly realized he must be parched. And starving.

I turned to one of the demons. "Could you get water and food from the kitchen?"

The demon looked at Roarke first, who nodded. "Always obey her."

Hmm. That was something. A smile tugged at my lips. I didn't know much about dating the Warden of the Underworld, but being given command over his demon minions had to be a step forward in our relationship.

"There's more you want to know," Cade said.

"Yes," Roarke said.

"But first, we can unchain you," I said. "All the bad things you did, they were at the bidding of the Shadows, right?"

Cade frowned. "Well, all the really bad things, yes. But I've cheated at cards and not called girls back and shit like that, so I can't blame it all on them."

Alton nodded. *Truth.*

"We'll just call that mildly bad," I said. "What I care about is that you mean us no harm."

"No! I definitely don't want to hurt you."

Alton nodded.

It took a few minutes, but we got all the chains and manacles off. Cade rubbed at the golden dampener charm around his wrist.

"That stays on for now," Roarke said.

Cade shrugged. "Got nowhere to go, anyway."

The demon who'd gone to get food returned. He was fast, and so was Cade. He made quick work of a glass of water and a sandwich, then looked at us.

"What are the Shadows' plans?" I asked. "How do they involve me?"

"They plan to open a massive portal to Earth. One that will allow thousands of demons to escape from hell onto Earth."

Shit. As Draka had predicted. "What is my role?"

"You play a key part, but I don't know the details."

Not great. "Where will the portal open?"

"I don't know. But I can lead you to them."

"We'll need you to," I said. "How many Shadows are there? And *who* are they?"

"There were six, though you killed one. They are a dark force, and very ancient. Not demon, not human, not any kind of supernatural I've ever known. I think they're evil."

"That's a given," I said.

"No, I mean, I think they are like, evil incarnate." He shrugged. "But that's just a theory. Only recently have they sought power. Now, they are the leaders of the demons who wish to be set free of the Underworld."

"Why do they want to be set free?" I asked. "I know that some come to Earth to act as mercenaries, but demons are from hell. That's their home. Most like it there. They have governments and lives and laws."

"True," Cade said. "Most *are* content, especially those who live within the various Kingdoms. It's not that different from Earth, really. There's good places and bad—heavens and hells—with demons and others just living their lives. And things have been better since Roarke began keeping the peace."

"Amongst the Kings of Hell, yes," Roarke said. "I don't have to worry about the heavens. Not my jurisdiction."

"And the Kings of Hell control their civilians," Cade said. "But there are outlaws who don't fit well into the Underworld, so they're trying to escape."

"Why don't they fit?" I asked.

"They're the worst of the worst—so bad that no King of Hell will let them into their Kingdom. And they don't want to be *in* the Kingdoms. They answer to no one and have existed on the periphery for centuries— millennia. When people think of evil demons, these are the ones. The baby eaters and skin-wearers."

"Of course." Roarke sighed. "And I haven't been able to control them because they aren't led by a King of Hell. They've existed in the Shadows, outside my control."

"Exactly," Cade said. "Though if you hadn't controlled the Kings of Hell, this would have happened sooner—with more demons discontent because of the wars."

"So now it's time for them to break free?" I guessed.

"Exactly. They've been planning to escape for over a thousand years, but they've never had a way to do it in massive numbers. Most just leave hell as mercenaries, getting an Earth-bound supernatural to free them in exchange for labor. Once on Earth, they go rogue and never return."

It was the whole reason I had been a mercenary—to track down the rogues. "But now they have a way for all of them to get out?"

"Yes. Because of the Shadows. They have the magic and the brains to orchestrate an escape. I think it is their purpose for existing."

"There have been more uprisings lately," Roarke said. "But I haven't been able to find the demons responsible. It's related, isn't it?"

Cade nodded. "I think so. Things have been getting more volatile lately. They sense that the Shadows have almost succeeded."

"Why now, though?" I asked. "It's been a thousand years."

"Because of you," Cade said. "You have the magic they need to escape. You're part of their plan."

"These Shadows are a suitable enemy for the Triumvirate," Alton said.

The FireSouls had been very interested in the Triumvirate, as my *deirfiúr* and I were called, when we'd visited them.

"This is your fated task, Del. You are meant to defeat them."

"I have to agree with him," Cass said.

"Yeah." I nodded. Alton made an excellent point. The Shadows and I were bound. They needed me to complete their goal, and I needed to defeat them.

"Which one cursed you, Cade?"

"I don't know. But I'd recognize him if I saw him. Not by sight, but by feel."

That wasn't helpful.

"Did you intend to curse me?" I asked. "Was that part of their plan?"

"Yes." Shame glinted in his eyes. "But I didn't want to! I swear."

"I know. When was this plan developed?"

"Just last week. After they saw Roarke with you. They had to draw you to them. They can't capture you themselves, because they are trapped in hell or near their portals and you're well-hidden. They hoped that stealing your Phantom dragon's source egg would work, but it did not."

"So they scrambled to develop a new plan," Roarke said.

Cade nodded. "Yes. They have demons scouting for Del, but her concealment charms protect her."

"I have good ones," I said. We'd bought them after we'd escaped the Monster, and I'd never gotten rid of them. Anyone who meant me harm couldn't scry for me.

"Right. And the Shadows know that. So they've been setting up traps to draw you to them."

"Eventually, I'd fall into one." As I had, by picking up Caden's curse.

"Exactly." Cade nodded sadly. "I'm so sorry that I cursed you."

"Don't worry about it. We'll find a way." *That hopefully doesn't involve killing you.* Because I was damned certain I couldn't do it. Sure, I could kill a demon or a monster intent on eating my head, but not another person.

Not a good person.

Not Roarke's *brother.*

I'd rather die. The only problem was—if I didn't defeat the Shadows, *everyone* would die. And the demons would turn the earth into hell.

So I'd just have to kill the Shadow who had cursed Cade and hope the effect trickled down to me, freeing me of the curse. And then I'd kill all the rest of the Shadows.

"I'll help you," Cade said.

Roarke nodded. "We're going to need you."

Later that night, Cass, Nix, and I sat on the upstairs landing, drinking boxed wine out of coffee mugs and spying on Roarke and Cade down in the living room. We couldn't hear them over the Allman Brothers that played on the stereo, so we weren't being super stalkers, but it was nice to watch them.

"They're so lucky," Nix murmured. She'd come by thirty minutes ago, after she'd done a bit of work at Ancient Magic.

"Yeah." I sipped my wine.

"I mean, he thought his brother was lost." Her voice was wistful. "But here he is."

I reached for her hand, knowing just what she was thinking. "We'll find your family."

Cass grabbed her other hand. "They might even be alive."

Hope lit up Nix's face. "You think?"

"Yeah, it's possible," I said.

"It's probable," Cass said. "One of us needs a happy ending with our families."

Nix's smile immediately fell. "Oh, I'm so sorry. That was thoughtless of me. You both already lost your families."

"I lost mine before I ever found them," I said.

"And we didn't lose all our family," Cass said. "We have each other."

Nix smiled. "We do."

After a while, Cass asked, "Do you have any idea what you'll do, Del?"

"You mean, about the curse?"

"Yeah."

"Hunt down the Shadows and kill them. Hopefully that will work." Worry tugged at my chest, stronger than ever. It was a demon with sharp claws, pulling and yanking. "I *can't* kill Roarke's brother."

"And you can't let the Shadows get control of you," Nix said. "Or worse will happen."

A prickle of sweat broke out on my skin at the very thought of it. "I know."

Demons breaking out onto Earth would be so much worse. Catastrophic on a level I couldn't begin to comprehend. Not only would they cause massive death and destruction—the Telenec demon wasn't the only flesh-eating variety—but they'd reveal supernaturals to the humans.

Then, not only would we be fighting demons, we'd be fighting humans as well. And there were so damned many humans. We relied on them. They built the infrastructure on which the world turned. Supernaturals used human money, roads, planes—everything. Most of us even blended into human cities.

It'd be the end of the freaking world as we knew it.

"Do you have any ideas?" Nix asked.

"Only one." Something strange fluttered in my chest, a visceral sensation. "I need to collect more powers. If I'm going to defeat so many Shadows, I need more gifts."

"I hate to be a downer," Nix said. "But you haven't even mastered your telekinesis yet. Should you steal more before you do that?"

Annoyance simmered. "I'll practice."

"You need to," Nix said. "Powers aren't any good if you can't use them."

"Will you take from demons or other supernaturals?" Cass asked.

"You mean take the gifts with my Phantom power or my FireSoul power?" I asked.

"Yeah."

"Phantom. It's easier—and less guilt inducing—to kill demons. I wouldn't know how to find supernaturals worth killing." And I didn't want to be the final judge of whether or not they deserved to die.

"Yeah, that's the hard part," Cass said. "You pretty much have to wait until their hands are around your throat before you make a move."

I squeezed her hand. Cass had killed her fair share of supernaturals to get her powers, but all had been after her life.

It was one reason I was grateful for my Phantom gift. I could grow my power with less guilt. It was easy to choose a demon who ate people, after all. I'd stay away from Roarke's contacts—demons like Jim Bob weren't fair game. They were good. Which made my job a bit harder. But I'd have to manage.

Nix looped her arm around my shoulders. "Just be careful, okay? Stealing powers is a slippery slope."

I nodded, but my mind was already on the hunt.

CHAPTER TEN

The next morning, I met Claire at P & P. I'd barely slept the night before, having spent the full six hours tossing and turning in my worry. The threat of the Shadows controlling me with the horror of killing Roarke's brother as being the only way to escape made it impossible to sleep.

I thought I'd been worried about my situation before…

I'd been naive.

Roarke was spending the day with his brother, questioning him about the last ten years, while I was with Claire, ready to hunt some demons. I'd called her last night, requesting as many hit jobs as she could get from her handler at the Order.

Before my "death," I'd been a mercenary, too, but I hadn't picked the work back up. I didn't exactly know how to explain my absence, so I'd decided not to explain at all. Ancient Magic had been doing well enough lately that we didn't need the money anymore. I'd never have guessed that I'd need a list of evil demons to target for reasons other than a paycheck.

Fortunately, I had Claire to call on.

"Ready?" Claire asked as I walked up to the coffee bar in the shop. She wore her leather battle gear, and her brown hair was pulled up in a ponytail.

I was so hyped up to get started—and so worried about what was coming—that I didn't even appreciate the scent of coffee, which was just plain weird.

"Hello?"

I blinked, startled, and met Connor's gaze. Apparently he'd been smiling and waving awhile, if the strain around his lips was any indication.

"Oh my gosh, I'm sorry." I frowned. "Was I ignoring you? I'm in my own world lately."

Connor shrugged. "It's cool. Lot on your mind. I hear you're going demon hunting with big sis today."

I nodded, then looked at Claire. "Ready?"

Though I'd tried not to sound too eager, I could hear it loud and clear in my voice.

Claire drained her coffee cup, pulled on her leather jacket, then smiled. "Yep."

As we hurried out of the shop, Claire dug some index cards out of her pocket and handed them to me. "Six jobs on the docket today."

"Six?" Excitement flared in me. That was a ridiculously high number.

"You said you wanted a lot." Claire grinned. "But don't worry. Some of those are wide calls. Other mercs may be after them, too. So if we don't finish, it's fine."

"Oh, I want to finish." I gave Scooter a longing glance, wishing I could ride my motorcycle, then followed Claire to her sleek sports car.

The engine roared as she pulled away from the curb. Claire had always been a real car fanatic.

"Pick which job you want to start with," Claire said.

I skimmed the cards. Unfortunately, there were no powers listed next to the demons' names, so we'd just have to hunt them down and see what they had.

"Let's try the Fortera demon," I said. "It says he stalks Hyde's Park in Darklane, looking for girls to…"

"I know what he's looking for." Claire grimaced and put her foot to the gas.

We pulled up to the park ten minutes later. The pace was wide and open, but in that familiar way of Darklane, everything looked vaguely gray. The huge oaks seemed to droop with the strain of growing here, where the sun shined half as bright.

We climbed out and made our way to the first tree, staying slightly behind it as we scanned the park. There were a couple joggers, but no one lying out on blankets or playing soccer, like you'd see in a regular park.

But then, there was nothing regular about Darklane.

It took nearly an hour of creeping around and keeping our eyes peeled, but finally we caught sight of the demon lurking in the bushes.

"He looks like any old peeping-Tom predator," I muttered.

"He is. But he doesn't stop at peeping."

I scowled, using my magic to reach out for his signature. I picked up a chill, but many powers carried that signature.

"Any idea what he is?" I peered at his form. I could just make out flashes of a dark coat and the occasional glint of his eyes to be sure he was actually in there.

He was a pro.

"No." Claire pointed across the path to the other bush. "He's got a partner."

I caught sight of a twitch of the bushes, just enough to see through a gap in the leaves. "Yep."

From down the path came the telltale sound of pounding footsteps. A moment later, a pretty woman appeared, jogging along in all black attire with flashy orange sneakers. She was just out enjoying her morning, while these monsters waited for her.

Rage boiled in my chest, pushing out the worry and fear that had been lodged in there like a hulking gargoyle.

"Sons a' bitches," I muttered.

"I'll take the far one, you take the close," Claire said.

"On it."

She gave the signal with her hand, a quick flick of the wrist, and we bolted from our spot behind the tree, startling the runner. I paid her no attention as I kept my gaze glued to the predator in the bush. He was so intent on his pretty prey that he didn't even see me coming until I was only a few feet away.

When he caught sight of me, he sprang up out of the bushes. I tackled him, sending him flying onto the asphalt path. His face scraped against the ground, and a sick satisfaction welled inside me.

Bastard deserved it. I was glad I couldn't read his intentions, because I was pretty sure they'd make me vomit.

"Get off!" the demon growled from beneath me.

I got a hint of his cold magic as I powered up an icicle and sent it through his back, not even bothering to turn him over.

He jerked and howled, but the sound was short.

I dragged him off toward the bushes to hide my Phantom form, only dimly realizing that I was acting like some kind of creepy predator myself.

A quick glance around revealed that the jogger had disappeared, and there was no one left to witness my Phantom form. I called upon the magic, letting it flow through me and turn my body pale blue and transparent.

The sight of my gray-tinged form made the worry rise back up in my chest.

I'd crush it soon, however, by stealing the power of the demon now bleeding out on the ground beneath me.

I flipped him over, ignoring the cold evil in his pain-stricken eyes, and reached out for his magic.

When the icy chill hit me, I faltered.

Ice magic?

"Damn it!" I shook him. He howled at the feel of my Phantom touch.

"What's wrong?" Claire asked. She'd finished off her demon and now stood above me.

"He has ice power." I stood and nearly growled down at him. "I already have that one."

"Don't want to catch the same Pokemon twice?" Claire asked.

"Can't." At my feet, the demon finally bled out and lay still. "I need new powers."

The monster in my chest clawed, worry feeding it. I'd *needed* this. Not just the power, but the kill. The act of taking it and proving that I could control my own fate. If only for a little while.

Claire pulled out her cell phone and snapped a pic of the demon. His form began to disappear a moment later.

"Ah, well. At least we got to save the girl." She showed me the picture. "And this will get me paid."

I nodded, trying to force my mind toward the thought of the girl. Just thinking of what might have happened to her made me shudder.

"Yeah." I nodded. "Glad I picked this job first, or we might have been too late."

"Fate."

"I think so." I just hoped fate was on my side in this whole deal.

"The demons are gone. Let's hit the next stop."

As we headed back to the car, I rifled through the cards. I slid into the passenger seat and said, "Let's head to the main road in Darklane. There's a demon who feeds off the pain of old people. He's been hitting up houses through their back entrances on Dimlight Alley."

But did I really want the power of such a monster?

Yes.

Beggars couldn't be choosers, and I didn't want to take power from anyone actually decent.

Claire nodded and gunned her engine, pulling away from the curb.

It was noon by the time we pulled up to the edge of Dimlight Alley. The houses on the main street all backed up to this narrow passage. The midday sun struggled to shine through the clouds, but it wasn't going to succeed. Not here. It was almost like the atmosphere of the place extended to the stratosphere.

The alley was even darker than the main street, so narrow that the shadows were deep and dark. Grime covered the walls, turning them pitch-black. Most of the windows were covered by dark curtains, and debris was piled outside of back doors.

We climbed out of the car just in time to see a shadow dart along the wall farther down the alley. Another followed him.

"Perfect way to break in," I said. It was so shadowed that they were well camouflaged, and there was no foot traffic like on the main street.

"Yep."

We hurried after the shadows, which turned out to be two large demons dressed all in black. The first slipped into an open kitchen window. The second tried to follow, but we were too quick.

He grunted as Claire dragged him off the windowsill. I hopped up and shimmied through. The kitchen was a disaster, the table flipped and plates shattered on the floor.

I raced through and into the narrow hall. The demon loomed in the close space, heading away from me.

I produced an icicle, firing without hesitation. He dodged, just in time, then whirled on me. He was over six feet tall and at least two hundred and fifty pounds. He growled, revealing long fangs.

I grimaced. Fangs meant biting. This monster likely planned to bite whatever poor person lived here.

The demon drew his sword and charged. I called on my telekinesis, attempting to hurl the side table in front of him. It barely wobbled.

Old faithful, then. I created another icicle, but he dodged this one, too. Damn, he was fast. He was almost upon me when I called upon my Phantom form. The chill raced through me as my limbs turned blue.

The demon hurtled through my ephemeral form. I shuddered and called my sword from the ether. Behind me, the demon made a retching noise, as if he hated the feel of me.

"I got more where that came from." I spun and leaped for him, wrapping my arms around his big form in a creepy hug.

He shuddered and yelled. I wasn't used to using the most common Phantom power—the ability to make those you touched relive their greatest fears and worst memories.

But I fed it into him, hoping to incapacitate him. He was so fast and so big—and so damned evil—that I had to play dirty.

He shuddered again, dropping to his knees as his yellow eyes rolled back in his head. I didn't know what would frighten a demon as strong and big as this one. I didn't want to.

When he toppled to his back, shaking, I followed him down and turned corporeal long enough to thrust my blade through his neck.

Blood sprayed up at me, warm and thick. I gagged as it coated my neck and face.

With bile rising in my throat, I resumed my Phantom form and reached for the demon's magic. This time, I got something unfamiliar. The feel of rain pelting my face, then sun, followed by a breeze.

Weather.

That was handy. I reached for his soul. The ephemeral thing tingled against my fingertips as I drew it out. Immediately, that sense of calm control rushed over me, driving out the disgust and worry and fear. As I absorbed his soul and his magic, my whole body buzzed.

I felt amazing.

The magic melded with mine, becoming one of an increasing number of signatures.

I reveled in the feeling of control, wanting to roll around in it forever.

Had Claire's demon disappeared yet, or could I possibly go steal his power as well?

A sound from behind me made me jump. I leaped up, leaving the body of the demon sprawled on the ground. I hoped it was another demon.

When I turned, I caught sight of an old man in a familiar blue velour tracksuit. His Gandalf beard reached to his waist and was tucked into the silky pants he wore. Spectacles glinted in the dim light.

"Aethelred?" The seer who had once helped me? I hadn't seen him since then.

"Delphine? What did you just do?"

I glanced down at my faded blue form. Shit. Quickly, I shifted back. "I didn't realize I was in your house."

"No, you were preoccupied."

"Um."

"What did you do here?"

Defensiveness prickled my spine. "You're the seer. Shouldn't you know?"

His pale eyes narrowed behind his spectacles. "No reason to get snappy."

Immediately, I hated myself. He was right. There was no need to act like this. "I'm sorry."

"It's all right. Who are they?"

"Forma demons." Claire's voice came from behind. She must have climbed in the window. "They like to…"

She trailed off, and I couldn't blame her. I wouldn't want to explain what they did, either.

"Ah, no. That is all right." Aethelred grimaced. "I know what they do."

"You didn't see them coming?" I asked.

He shook his head. "No. I scry for danger, but I found nothing because I was never at risk. Fate decreed that you would stop them. Thank you."

"Glad to be of service." Claire saluted. "Though perhaps you should have scried for damage to your kitchen, because I think that guy knocked some things over."

A pink glow stained Aethelred's cheeks. "No, ah, that was a jazzercise episode gone a bit awry. I was just returning to clean it up."

So *that's* why he always wore tracksuits. I grinned, but didn't ask more. He clearly didn't want to talk about it.

"It's lunchtime. Can I feed you? It's the least I can do." He nodded to the demon's body, which wasn't disappearing. "As soon as his body goes away."

I didn't know how to tell him it wouldn't go away because I'd stolen its soul, but my stomach answered for me by rumbling.

"We'll take care of the body," Claire said. "He's, um, a rare type of demon who doesn't disappear after death. And a rain check on the food, but thank you."

"How about something to go?" Aethelred asked. "I'll make sandwiches. And give you a wet paper towel." He nodded at the blood on my face.

Now *that* was something I could use. The scent of the blood was making me queasy. "Thank you."

We hauled the body down the hall and back out the window. While Aethelred made sandwiches inside, we stood out in the alley below his window. I wiped off with the paper towel while Claire incinerated the body.

"Get anything good?" she asked.

"Weather."

"Oh, that is good."

The body was gone by the time Aethelred handed two paper sacks out the window. "Turkey and cheese."

I took them. "Thank you." It seemed a shame to waste this opportunity. "Could I ask you—have you seen anything new about me? I'd be happy to pay."

"And well you should be." Yep, there was the curmudgeonly Aethelred I remembered. "Just give me a moment."

While hanging out the window, he closed his eyes. His magic surged around him. The scent of cinnamon grew strong. Something in the air calmed. It was almost trance-like. When his eyes popped open, I almost jumped.

"You're going to fail." His tone was sharp.

"What?" My stomach dropped.

"You have many goals, all important. One will fail. Quite dreadfully."

Chills raced over my skin, followed quickly by a sheen of sweat. "What should I do?"

He shrugged. "What would you normally do?"

"Try to stop it. But I don't even know what I'm going to fail at."

"I'm sure you can guess."

Among many things, sure. Fail to stop the Shadows. Fail to save the world. Fail to cure my curse. Fail to not kill Roarke's brother. There were a *lot* of bad things I could fail to do.

"I really need a clue," I begged. "Anything."

He shook his finger. "You know how this works. I don't see all, but—"

"What you do see is true." Dread was like oil in my stomach making me ill.

"Yes. That'll be two hundred dollars."

Shit. Did I even have cash on me? My hands shook as I tried to search my pockets, but Claire's hand appeared in front of me, thrusting out a wad of bills.

"Thanks for nothing, pal," she said.

"That was hardly nothing!" Indignation laced Aethelred's voice.

Claire hoisted her bag of sandwiches. "Then thanks for the sandwiches." She grabbed my arm. "Come on, we've got another job."

I followed her down the alley, my mind racing. "What am I going to fail at?"

"I don't know, but I fail at stuff all the time. What's one more thing?"

"Yeah, but the things on my plate are pretty huge lately."

She stopped, turning toward me. Her gaze was sad. "I know. And you're trying your best. We're all trying. We can do this."

Could we? Whatever control high I'd gotten from killing that demon had faded, replaced by the gnawing worry and fear. Shadows, Cade, curse, end of the world, queen of the demons.

All of it was just too much.

But I couldn't break down, no matter how badly I wanted to.

I sucked in a ragged breath. "Come on. We've got a demon to find."

The rest of the day went quickly. We forfeited one demon to another mercenary, who'd gotten there before us, so by the time we reached a dimly lit bar at the dingiest corner of Darklane, I was ready to do some damage.

"Split up?" Claire asked at the door to the bar.

"Yeah." We wouldn't have long inside before someone booted us out. This place was a hell of a lot shadier, and a hell of a lot more private, than the gambling den from the other day. Mordaca's name wouldn't help us here.

We hurried inside. Smoke choked me almost immediately, along with a cacophony of dark magic signatures. Fortunately, the place was crowded with bodies. Claire and I split up immediately, pushing our way through the crush. BO and perfume overwhelmed the scent of magic—these demons were here to get their freak on.

Our target was supposed to be a tall, slender Whispa Demon with pale skin and no eyes. Just imagining it made me shudder.

The bar was crowded, standing room only, but it took only seconds to determine he wasn't in the room. Though there were some creepy looking figures, there was nothing as bad as the Whispa demon.

I shoved my way toward the back of the bar, hoping to find a kitchen or supply closet.

"What the hell are you doing here?" growled an unfamiliar voice from behind me.

I sent my elbow into his gut and hurried on. My desire to make another kill and collect another power was almost choking me now. I hadn't been able to get Aethelred's words out of my head all afternoon. They'd just grown and grown and grown.

And he was *never wrong.*

There were two doors at the back. My dragon sense pulled me toward the one on the right. I tried the handle, but it was locked. So I fed my ice power into it, loading it up until the thing was brittle as glass. All I had to do was yank hard, and the thing shattered.

When I opened the door, the first thing I saw was a demon looming over a chair. It was tall and spindly, with long horns and pale, pale skin. No eyes. There was a figure in the chair, but I had eyes only for the demon. Bloodlust—power lust—roared in my head.

I wound up an icicle and hurled it at the thing. This time, the weapon found its mark. The demon was either too slow or too absorbed to notice it coming.

When the icicle sank into the beast's skinny back, it stiffened, shrieking in the most horrible voice.

Claire burst into the room behind me, gasping. "I'll get the person."

She raced for the figure in the chair as I hurled myself at the demon, leaping onto its back. I barely registered Claire dragging the victim from the room and slamming the door behind her. I shot another icicle through the chest of the demon.

Hunger surged through me as the life faded out of the monster, disgust on its heels. What was I turning into?

Music and voices continued to blare outside as I watched the life quickly fade from the demon. Blood dripped from its mouth, coating fangs that had probably just been sunk into its victim's neck. This wasn't a vampire, but it was damned close.

I reached out for its magic, trembling. When the ephemeral thing vibrated against my fingertips, I sighed, pulling it free. Once again, that comforting sense of control welled over me. It was only after I'd fully absorbed the gift that I even stopped to discover what I had taken.

Sound. The gift of muffling or creating sound.

Strange, but handy.

It was probably how this monster crept up on its target.

Was I the monster now?

No. I shook the thought away. I needed the power. More than that, at this very moment, I needed the calm sense of control that came with taking it.

The door creaked open, and Claire's voice sounded. "You okay?"

"Yeah." My voice was shaky as I climbed to my feet. In fact, my limbs were also pretty damned shaky.

Claire reached me, her expression concerned. "You don't look all right. Your eyes are pretty bright. How's the power-taking? Aren't you worried about taking too much?"

I shook my head. "Cass has a ton of powers and she's fine. I'm fine, too."

Skepticism flashed across Claire's face, a familiar frown.

"How's the victim?" I asked, wanting to distract her. I was also genuinely concerned. I remembered seeing blood on her as she'd been dragged away.

"Fine. A few bites, pretty shaken up, but she'll be okay eventually. What power did you get off the demon?"

"Sound. I think I can make it or muffle it."

"Not bad." She pulled her phone from her pocket and checked the time. "Then that should be enough for the day. It's eight and we should quit."

We were used to working late hours. But from her tone, it was obvious what was wrong. She was worried about all the powers I was taking. Or that I was starting to act weird.

Maybe I was.

But these were extenuating circumstances.

"Ready?" Claire asked.

"Yeah." I let her drive me back to my place, though I desperately wanted to hunt for the last two demons on her note cards.

When she dropped me off in front of Ancient Magic, I leaned down so I could see through the car window. "Thanks again for today. You're a great friend."

She smiled, but her brow was wrinkled in concern. "You just take care to practice those powers."

"I will." I watched her drive off, then raced up into my apartment, trying to practice my new sound power so that Nix couldn't hear me run by her place. It muffled my footsteps a bit, but not totally. Like Claire said, I'd need more practice.

Fortunately, Nix didn't hear me, and I was able to grab my keys and hop on Scooter, tearing away from the curb in record time.

I'd memorized Claire's note cards, and there were still two demons left to find.

CHAPTER ELEVEN

The first demon was a bust. Another mercenary had gotten to him. Disappointment was bitter and tinged with desperation.

But the second was sitting in a tree outside a kid's window in a pretty little neighborhood at the edge of town. Inside, I could see a five-year-old sitting on a window seat, playing with a doll.

Fucking creeper.

I shivered as I watched him, as much from cold as from anticipation. I hadn't even stopped to properly clean my face after it'd been sprayed with demon blood. I'd been too excited to get out here.

A group of chattering teenagers ambled down the street. One was practicing his fire magic, tossing a glowing ball up into the air to impress the girl next to him.

Shit. Witnesses. I didn't need witnesses. Especially not more kids.

The demon caught sight of the teenagers. Briefly, his eyes flared.

Was he going to go for them?

He began to shimmy down the tree. From his haste, I'd bet he was going to run for it. Otherwise he'd wait till the teenagers were below him and strike. But there were too many of them, and fire kid could light him up. Anyway, his sort was a coward, waiting till a five-year-old was asleep to sneak in and eat him.

Disgust rose in my belly, competing with the desire to make the kill.

I couldn't let this asshole get away.

I wound up an icicle, raising my hand to throw.

Something gripped my arm.

I gasped, spinning. Nix was holding on to me.

"What the hell?" I demanded.

Beside her, Cass waved her hand. The ground next to the tree rose up and grabbed the demon, then swallowed him up to his neck until only his head stuck out of the earth.

"It's time to go home," Nix said.

Cass called Claire on her phone, stating our location and problem.

"But I'm working." Desperation quivered in my muscles. When would I find another clearly evil demon again? This was the last one on Claire's list! "I'm collecting powers, just like we agreed on."

"No." Cass nodded, her gaze soft. "You're freaking out and going nuts. You were supposed to quit with Claire hours ago."

"We hadn't finished." My voice quivered.

Okay, yeah. Maybe I was freaking out a little.

Cass wrapped her arm around my neck and pulled me close for a hug. "Come on. Let's go home."

I drew in a shuddery breath, trying to calm the rising panic in my chest.

I was never like this. Calm and cool was my deal—not this freaked-out, nearly crying mess I'd become.

Nix squeezed my hand. "Let's go."

"Yeah. Yeah, okay." I followed them to Cass's car. Someone could come get Scooter later. Right now, I needed my *deirfiúr.*

"So what's the deal?" Cass asked.

I stared down into my mug of red wine, letting the comfort of my trove seep into my pores. We sat on an old couch in the middle of my trove, surrounded by piles of books and lucky talismans. This was where we always came whenever one of us was having a bad time. Since it was my turn for things to go to shit, we were in my trove.

I sipped the wine, appreciating my friends' patience. It took me time to sort through the mess in my head, anyway.

"Stealing the demons' powers makes me feel in control," I finally said.

"Yeah, I can understand that," Cass said.

"But you already are in control," Nix said. "You don't need to go doing that kind of thing."

I stiffened. "I only choose evil demons. And I *was* a mercenary, if you recall. It's not exactly out of character for me."

Nix nodded sympathetically. "No, you're right. I get it. I just mean that you're using it in the wrong way. To feel better for a while. I mean, you were sneaking out like an addict after a fix."

Her description was so apt that I couldn't argue. That'd just make me look guiltier. And hell, I *was* guilty. Of freaking out at the very least.

"It's just that if I don't kill Roarke's brother, the one who cursed me, then I'm susceptible to the Shadows' control. Then *really* bad things will happen. But I *can't* kill Roarke's brother. And I *can't* become susceptible to the Shadows."

"No, those are both awful," Nix said.

I nodded. "So my only hope is to be strong enough to be sure I can kill a Shadow."

"You *can*," Cass said.

"And I saw Aethelred today." The words spilled out of me. "He said I'm going to fail at one of my goals. An important goal."

There was silence from both sides of the couch. It didn't make me feel better, but at least they were taking me seriously.

Finally, Cass said, "I can see why you freaked out."

Nix smiled sympathetically. "Yeah, you've got some pretty important goals lately."

"Exactly." I let out a shuddery laugh, then sipped my wine.

"But you're not alone," Nix said.

"I know. I have you guys."

"And all our power," Cass said. "Between all of us, we have a pretty insane arsenal. Whatever the Shadows throw at us, we can defeat it."

"Not according to Aethelred," I said.

"Even if he's right—"

"He is," I interrupted.

"Yeah." Cass nodded. "He's right. He's always right. You're going to fail at something. But just one thing. You have a *lot* of things you need to accomplish. We'll manage the rest. Together."

"But you need to quit going rogue and stealing powers," Nix said.

"It was just one night," I said. But I could hear the weaselly complaint in my voice. I was better than that.

"We don't have any more nights to spare." Nix sniffed deeply. "And it seems like you had quite a night. Two new powers?"

I nodded. "Sound and weather."

"Those are good. But you need to practice."

Nix, always with the practice. But she was an excellent conjurer. Practice had served her well.

"Okay," I said. "No more stealing—unless the demons drop into my lap. And I'll practice."

"Now." Nix pointed to the stack of books in front of me. "You're still pretty shit with your telekinesis, and tomorrow is going to be a big day."

She was right. My failed attempt to launch a table at the demon today was evidence of that.

I called upon my telekinesis power. I held it inside myself, just under the surface, getting used to it.

Nix fluttered her hand. "Now lift the books."

My first attempt was a disaster. They thudded to the ground after hovering for only a moment. But I pushed myself harder. I could do this. It was just another power.

We spent the evening practicing my telekinesis and gift over sound. Not the weather, though. I didn't want to ruin my books with an impromptu rain shower. After an evening with my *deirfiúr* and several hours of practice, I was feeling a lot better.

Still freaked-the-hell-out, but a lot better. Apparently gaining control of my magic could feel almost as good as taking it. The whole process was harder, but with Cass and Nix to help, at least I had company. And backup.

Finally, around 2:00 a.m., we were exhausted, and half a box of wine was gone.

"Thanks, guys," I murmured. "You're the best."

"We're family." Nix reached for my hand.

"Family." Cass grabbed my other hand. "And whatever is coming at us, we'll meet it together."

Late that night, after Cass and Nix had gone back to their apartments, Roarke knocked on my door. I knew it was him before I even opened it.

As soon as I saw him, I threw my arms around his waist. He was warm and strong against me, a grounding presence that felt better than stealing any power in the world.

He hugged me back, kissing the top of my head. "You doing all right?"

"Yeah," I mumbled against his chest. "Had a bit of a slip today, but I'm doing all right now."

"Want to tell me about it?"

I didn't, not really. But not because I didn't trust him. More because I was embarrassed. But weren't those the things you should fess up to if you wanted to be in a relationship? I needed to own my mistakes, or I'd make them again. "Sure. But let's do it in bed. I'm beat."

We snuggled into my bed. Roarke was almost too big for the queen mattress, but we made it work. Once the covers were up and the world was blocked out, I snuggled against him and told him about the day.

When I finished, he nodded. I felt the movement against my head, which rested on his shoulder. "I can see how you might do something like that."

"Diplomatic."

He shrugged. "It just makes sense, is all. But you're also making better decisions now, so it's okay."

"I hope so."

"We can do this, Del."

"Yeah." I couldn't think about it. "How is your brother?"

"Good." I could hear the smile in his voice. "Very good. We spent the day together. He told me about what to expect tomorrow when we go to the Shadows' Underworld headquarters."

"Did he have a lot of valuable info?"

"Depends on how lucky we get." He told me what Caden knew, but it wasn't much. Most of Caden's value was in leading us there. We'd have to blindly face the challenges that awaited.

"We should remove the dampening charm," I said. "He'll need to be able to fight alongside us."

"Yeah. You're right."

"All this talk of battles to come is making me want to appreciate my life." I looked up and grinned at him.

He smiled. "Yeah? Got any idea how you want to do that?"

"I can think of a few ways." I leaned up and kissed him.

He groaned and pulled me on top of him. I clutched at his strong shoulders, straddling him as I devoured his kiss. My mind buzzed with pleasure as he rolled me over.

"Yes." I gasped as his mouth traced down my neck and over my shoulders, which were revealed by my tank top. Why had I even bothered wearing clothes to bed?

In the end, it didn't matter. Roarke knew just how to get me out of them, and I enjoyed every second.

Later that night, after I regained my senses and Roarke had drifted to sleep, I snuck away to my trove. I sat on the couch, begging Draka to come to me. I didn't know how to summon her—only that she came when I needed her—so I used my desperation.

Because even with my friends at my back, this task seemed potentially insurmountable. I was used to obvious problems with obvious solutions—find the treasure, kill the demon. That kind of thing.

This was totally out of my league.

But Draka never came. Apparently my situation wasn't dire enough. Which I couldn't say I agreed with.

So I did what I always did when I had a big, dangerous job coming up. I combed through my trove and selected the best of my lucky talismans for the job. In truth, I doubted I needed anything other than Roarke's bracelet. But it was soothing to comb through my collection, selecting necklaces and a shirt that would buoy me against what was to come.

I wasn't stupid—I knew it was up to me to save the day. But sometimes, a lucky talisman could make the difference. If only in my confidence.

CHAPTER TWELVE

"Wow, this is nothing like their headquarters in Germany." I looked out across the golden hills of sand as the sun beat down upon my face. Sweat rolled down my spine, and I shrugged out of my leather jacket, grateful for the tank top I wore beneath.

Roarke had just transported us all through an Underpass to a desert in Egypt. A small, beaten-down pyramid had been our exit point, though we still had a ways to go, according to Cade.

"That's just one of their locations," Cade said. "It was an ideal place to store Draka's source egg. But their actual headquarters are in the Underworld. There are several portals that lead to that Underworld, one of them at the castle in Germany, but that is too well guarded."

"Agreed," Nix said. "This should have no guards?"

"It never has before." Cade shielded his eyes with his hand and looked out across the sand. "This portal is at an abandoned settlement called Zerzura. It's in an oasis. When I'd come before, demons would escort me. But I remember how to get there."

"Zerzura?" Nix asked. "Isn't that a mythical lost city?"

"Not lost anymore," Cade said.

Worry tugged at me. 'Lost' cities were usually lost because they were so well protected that no one ever found them.

"Do you know what kind of protections might be guarding it?" I asked.

"None when I came with the demons."

That didn't make me feel too much better.

Claire pointed across the sand to a group of small dots heading toward us. "Looks like our rides are almost here."

After a few moments, they were close enough to make out shapes. A herd of camels led by three men. Demon contacts of Roarke's, as usual. One for each of us—myself, Roarke, Cass, Aidan, Nix, Connor, Claire, and Cade. Everyone had insisted on coming, though I'd tried to dissuade Connor and Claire. They'd risked their lives for us enough. They wouldn't hear of it, though.

The herd of camels finally stopped in front of us, and the three demons, all dressed in white robes, swung off and approached Roarke. They spoke a language I didn't recognize, but soon we were saddled up and trotting across the desert.

Cass leaned over on her camel and said, "This reminds me of that pyramid we raided for the dampening charm."

I grinned. "That was a tough one. That sphinx scared the crap out of me."

"Me too." Cass laughed.

We rode for hours, the sun beating down upon us. At some point, I named my camel Iago, but he didn't seem to care. I admired his gleaming golden fur. If I hadn't been dressed in black, we'd have blended well into the golden sand.

We were close to Zerzura by the time the air started to feel weird. Only a mile, according to Cade.

"Something's wrong. Can you—"

A low, rumbling roar cut off Nix's words. Around me, my friends stiffened, and the camels snorted nervously. Ahead, the sand began to shimmer and roll, rising high into the air, swirling madly. It created a wall around us.

"What's this, Cade?" Roarke demanded.

"I don't know!"

Had Cade betrayed us?

No. Alton had determined that Cade was telling the truth and he was on our side. And I trusted him.

But whatever magic was possessing the sand, it wasn't in our favor. The golden granules coalesced to form a massive snake. It was a sandstorm with shape, and it was rolling right toward us. The beast was at least two hundred meters long and fifty meters high. Long fangs made of sand protruded from the snake's mouth.

My camel bucked, but unlike in Peru, I was ready. I clung to it, gazing at the sand snake in horror. Another rose up next to it, this one even bigger. Both were headed straight for us.

Cass hurled a massive fireball at the snake, which was only fifty yards away now. Aidan joined her. Together, they shot huge jets of flame that seared my skin.

But the snake wasn't afraid.

And there was no way to kill a monster made of sand.

Unless...

I called upon my new power over the weather. It was rusty—the most I'd ever practiced was to form a few clouds early this morning. But desperation made me willing to try anything.

The feel of wind and sun and rain welled within me, a strange feeling.

"Hurry up, Del!" Nix cried.

I released my magic, hurling it toward the sky and demanding that it rain, envisioning a monsoon. In the distance, thunder cracked. Though the sun shone brightly, clouds formed in an instant, and rain began to pour. Millions of huge droplets spilled down from the sky, nearly blinding me.

Most importantly, they drowned the snake, melting its sand-form back into the earth. It was a half-melted pile within moments, writhing in its death throes.

"Keep going!" Connor cried.

I poured more magic into the air, begging the rain to continue. Rain splashed down, obliterating the snakes and turning the ground to sandy slush.

Finally, when the monsters were nothing more than puddles, I pulled back on my magic. The rain stopped immediately.

"Wow." I panted. That was wild.

"Well done," Roarke said.

"That's a handy new talent," Cass said. "You saved our hides there."

I nodded, somewhat stunned by the power of being able to call up such an enormous rainstorm. The air steamed as the desert sun heated the wet sand at our camels' feet. Their soaking fur began to give off steam, and my clothes heated quickly. The air became thick with humidity.

"Let's keep going." I nudged my camel with my knee.

The camels plodded through the slushy sand, which grew firmer as the sun dried it.

"That's never happened before?" Roarke asked Cade.

"No." Cade glanced around. "But we're close. It's normally a four-hour camel ride."

"The demons may have had some kind of protection charms that allowed them to pass through any enchantment protecting the settlement," Cass said.

"I'm thinking it's likely," Cade said. "I never paid much attention. They only started allowing me at their headquarters in the past year. By that time, I was fully under their control. The curse had totally taken over my mind."

"I wonder what's coming next, then?" I muttered to Roarke.

"Wish I knew."

"We'll just have to be ready," Connor said.

Though we were supposed to be close to our destination, the rest of the ride seemed to take forever. As soon as I spotted a speck on the horizon, the heat of the sun seemed to dial up to a thousand degrees. Sweat popped up on my skin, only to be evaporated a half second later. My clothes dried fully in the space of a few seconds, and the air felt so dry that my skin itched.

"This is weird," Cass muttered.

I started to pant, and my vision began to blur.

"It's too hot." Cade squinted up at the sun. "This is unnatural. It used to be hot, but this…"

"I'll try—" I didn't have energy to speak. I was woozy as I called upon my magic, managing to form a few clouds in the sky. But they were no match for the sun, which blazed right through them. This wasn't weather—this was enchantment.

I fumbled for the water bottles in my pack. We'd each brought three, and everyone seemed to be of the same mind. I cranked the top off the first one, then held it out toward Iago's head. He turned his neck and delicately plucked the water bottle from my hand, his big front teeth clutching the small bottleneck. He tilted his head up and let the liquid pour down his throat. As he drank, I sucked one down, too, then handed the last to Iago.

Had I known I'd be sharing with a camel, I'd have brought more. These guys could really drink.

After everyone had polished off their waters, the camels stumbled along for twenty more yards. No one spoke as the heat continued to increase.

Within minutes, my mouth had dried out almost entirely as the dry air sucked the moisture from my body. My tongue was a dry brick in my mouth. We hadn't brought nearly enough water.

"This isn't right," Cass slurred.

Iago stumbled, affected by the heat.

If it was getting to this desert animal, we were screwed. And the oasis was still so far away. Around us, the air shimmered. We were trapped in some kind of pocket of deadly heat.

"Hang on, guys." Nix's voice sounded far away. Her magic swelled lightly on the air.

Suddenly, a big bucket of water appeared in front of Iago. He bent and lapped it up greedily. Through hazy vision, I saw Nix lead her camel around, stopping at each person. She handed out gallon jugs of water and golf umbrellas.

"Thanks." I panted. I took mine gratefully, popping open the umbrella. The shade helped immensely, but it was the water that really saved my life. Literally.

For a while, the only sound was that of the camels slurping and the rest of us chugging water. Nix replenished the camels' buckets four times before they were satisfied.

Finally, we were recovered enough to keep riding, but we needed to stop three more times before we finally made it out of the enchanted heat bubble. Twice, I'd started to keel over, and Roarke had pushed me upright. It happened to each of us at some point as our bodies gave up in the heat.

But as soon as my camel stepped through the shimmery air that marked the edge of the enchanted area, the temperature difference was immediate. Though still hot, it wasn't kill-you-in-ten-minutes-hot.

I sagged over Iago's back, panting. Slowly, my vision cleared. We had another water break, and it was five minutes before anyone could speak.

"Jeez, Nix, you saved our bacon big time," Connor said.

"No kidding." Roarke frowned back at the shimmery trap. "We would have died without water."

Nix laughed, sounding out of breath. "Conjuring water and umbrellas seems kinda lame, but in that heat..."

"Life saving," I said.

"That was bad." Cade's worried gaze was glued to the oasis, which was still far off on the horizon. "And I have no idea what's coming."

Cass shrugged. "We normally have no idea what's coming, so it's nothing new."

"And at least you know the way." My dragon sense hadn't worked, more the pity.

"Let's keep going." Roarke nudged his camel into a trot.

Fortunately, we hit no more snags in the desert. By the time we arrived at the edge of the brilliant green oasis, I was eager to get out of the sun. Right before we reached the trees, the camels pulled up short, standing in a perfectly straight line.

As if there was a protective barrier.

"I think I see why Zerzura has been a lost city," I muttered.

"I do remember this," Cade said. "We would pause here while a demon would chant something in a foreign language."

"I don't suppose you remember it?" Roarke asked.

Cade shook his head. "No."

"No problem." Roarke climbed down from his camel, shifting quickly into his demon form. His dark wings flared as he stepped up to the boundary, feeling for it with outstretched hands.

Once he found it, he braced himself, then pulled back his fist and slammed it forward. It crashed against the invisible barrier, sending brilliant white lines streaking across the air like cracked glass. It took five more massive blows before the barrier shattered. It was like a hole in an invisible dome, only apparent because the edges looked like clear, jagged glass.

Roarke stepped back, and we passed by, single file. I glanced behind to see Roarke shift to human, then jump on his ride and follow us through. The camels plodded into the jungle, weaving expertly between palm trees as the verdant growth thickened.

"I sure hope there's nothing waiting for us in here," Cass muttered.

"Same."

We reached a brilliant blue pool without problem. Animals had chittered at us from their hiding places amongst the leaves, but they hadn't attacked. No charms had ignited against us, perhaps because the whole oasis was considered to be part of Zerzura. I'd caught sight of decayed white stone buildings, but there were no threats.

"This is it." Cade gestured to the beautiful blue pool and the destroyed white building on the other side. The water was crystal clear and sparkled in the sunlight. "That's an ancient temple. This culture worshiped the Shadows."

I shuddered, suddenly glad their time had come to an end. Their temple was in better shape than the Incate village had been, but not by much.

"Where exactly is the portal?" I asked.

"See that platform over there?" Cade pointed across the water to a large flat rock that butted up against the water like a deck. A cliff rose on the side opposite the water, and six ornately carved stones bordered the glittering blue pool. "It's over there."

We climbed off our camels. I scratched mine on the neck and met his big brown eyes. "You hang out for a while. If we're not back in a day, head home."

Iago nodded as if he understood me. Even if he didn't, he'd find his way home. Roarke had said the camels knew how to get back.

We walked around the pool, following a stone path that hadn't been overtaken by the jungle.

"This is a good adventure," Connor said. His bag of potion bombs was slung across his back. "Nice to get out of P & P every now and then."

I grinned, hoping that we wouldn't actually need his help. But since we were going into the lair of my greatest enemy—and I was still cursed to obey their orders—that was a long shot.

We followed Cade up onto the big stone platform. Up close, I could see that the cliff was a stone wall covered by vines. Cade walked up to the wall and pressed his hands against it, clearly expecting something to happen.

When nothing did, his shoulders sagged. Mine did, too.

"There's a problem," Roarke said.

"Yeah." Cade turned to us. "That's the portal. But it didn't open."

"The demons who brought you here must have had a key," Aidan said.

Cade frowned. "I never saw one."

"Wouldn't have had to be obvious." Aidan inspected the wall, pushing aside vines.

"That just means we have to figure out how to open the portal." Though the delay wasn't helpful, a grin still tugged at the corners of my lips. I liked a challenge. "Let's look for clues."

Everyone began poking around the stone platform, inspecting the six intricately carved stones that stood like sentries at the edge. But it was the flat stone wall that really interested me.

I began to tear away the vines. Roarke helped me, his big hands making quicker work. Eventually, everyone joined in. By the time we were done, I was sweating. The pool behind me was so tempting, but a cheerful swim wasn't on the agenda.

We stepped back and examined our handiwork.

"Well, that's definitely a door." I studied the lines etched in the flat stone wall. There was also a ten-pointed star within the outline of the door.

"Yep," Cass said. "But how do we open it?"

Roarke stepped up, shifting into his demon form. He pulled back his fist and slammed it into the stone.

Nothing happened.

He tried two more times. The third time, magic radiated out from the stone, but the portal didn't open.

He turned to face us. "I can't do it. There's some kind of magic that needs to be ignited."

That wasn't a huge surprise, really. This whole place screamed ceremonial site.

I studied the star and door outline, then turned around and examined our surroundings. We were in an opening in the oasis, the sun beating down on the pond and our little ceremonial site. There were six pillars at the edges of the platform, creating a semicircle around the stone wall with the carving.

A dark stain dripped down the vertical side of each of the pillars. At the bottom of each pillar, there was a line carved in the stone floor. Six lines extended to the middle of the platform, right under my feet. They joined in the middle in a depression. One wider line, the indention at least an inch deep, extended to the door carved in the flat wall.

Hmmm. That was no coincidence.

I walked to one of the pillars and stood on my tiptoes. A shallow indention was carved in the top of each. A little notch was carved in the stone that would have allowed whatever was poured in the indention to flow out one side.

"I think they used fire." I turned to face my friends. "Come look at this."

I showed them the indention in the top of the pillar, which led to the stain that ran down the pillar. "I think they poured something flammable in this indention. It stained the stone as it flowed over the edge, down the pillar, then followed the channel carved in the ground to the door."

"Is this anything like what you saw when you were here?" Roarke asked Cade.

"No. But the supernaturals may have had their own way of opening the portal that was different from the demons."

"Very possibly, yes," I said.

Nix nodded. "Then let's try."

"It's worth a shot." I looked at her. "Can you conjure oil or something?"

"No problem." Nix conjured several jugs of oil and passed them around.

We filled the indentions in the tops of the pillars, letting them overflow. As expected, the oil poured down the front side of the pillar, following the indentions carved in the stone floor. Apparently, the ground was slightly slanted, allowing the oil to travel quickly to the central pool and then down the one wider indention toward the portal door.

"This is cool," Cass said. "We're recreating history. Just like those guys who repeat battles from the Civil War on Saturday afternoons, then go get ice cream."

"Except we're trying to break into an Underworld," I said.

"Yeah." Cass frowned. "There's definitely a higher probability of a terrible death."

"But if we make it out, I'll definitely buy you ice cream." I grimaced and grinned at the same time, both horrified and wanting to laugh.

"Ready to light this thing up?" Aidan asked.

I moved to be closer to the portal. Everyone except Aidan and Cass followed.

"Try it now," I said.

Aidan and Cass conjured three fireballs each, directing them at the pillars. The flames flew through the air, each fireball landing on top of a pillar at the same time. Flames burst to life on top of each pillar. The flames raced down the side of the pillar and across the ground, following the oil.

The pool of oil in the middle of the platform blazed six feet tall. Heat singed my skin. I kept my sight riveted to the flame as it followed the stream of oil to the door.

When it reached the portal, magic took over. The flame turned blue and bright, racing across the outline of the door and lighting up the star. The glow was so strong that it hurt my eyes. It spread across the stone, making the whole thing glow blue.

"I think it's working," Roarke murmured.

"This is what it looked like when the demons took me through," Cade said.

"Then let's go." Roarke stepped forward. "It may only last as long as the flame. Partner up."

I reached for Nix's hand. Roarke and I were usually the only ones who could help other people cross into the Underworld, but this time, Cade could lend a hand, given that he was half demon like Roarke.

Nix gripped my hand, and we stepped forward. Roarke, holding Aidan's hand, stopped us.

"Insist on going first?" I asked.

He grinned, then walked through with Aidan. Nix and I followed immediately, letting the ether suck us into hell.

CHAPTER THIRTEEN

As soon as I stepped out into the barren hellscape beyond, I gasped. The earth was black as pitch, the sky a deep, dark gray. A moon gleamed in the distance, barely shedding any light at all on our surroundings.

"Oh yeah, this is hell," Nix said.

Cade stepped through a moment later, bringing Claire. He nodded. "This is it."

"It sucks," I said.

He shrugged. "It's the official headquarters of a group called the Shadows who are evil incarnate."

I nodded. "Yeah, okay. It fits."

While Roarke and Cade returned to Earth for Cass and Connor, I took in our surroundings. Cade had told us that the actual headquarters was about five miles away, and in the gloom, I couldn't see it.

"I'm worried about what's coming," Nix said.

"Me too," Claire said. "Cade clearly hasn't seen everything this world has to offer."

The rest of our party joined us a second later, and I turned to Cade. "Your demon escorts protected you from the enchantments guarding the oasis. Do you know if there are any here?"

He shook his head. "I was always escorted. So there could be anything."

My stomach sank. We'd come prepared for obstacles, but who knew what the Shadows would send at us?

"Might as well get a move on, then." I gestured to Cade. "If you'll lead the way?"

"Hang on." For the first time ever, his magic swirled around him. It was vaguely similar to Roarke's, though a bit weaker. The tornado of black dust that enclosed him was a lighter color, as well. More of a gray.

But when he'd finally shifted, the resemblance was uncanny. He was slightly smaller and his wings were a different shape, but he was clearly Roarke's brother.

"It might be best for everyone to shift into their strongest form," Cade said.

As Roarke and Aidan changed, I debated adopting my Phantom form. But Roarke and Cade blended into the dark. Even Aidan had turned into a black griffin, though he usually favored gold.

"I'm going to wait to shift," I said. "I'll light up the night in my Phantom form."

"Smart," Roarke said.

The rest of us stayed human, though I could tell that Cass was ready to shift at a moment's notice if necessary. Because she was a Mirror Mage, not a natural-born shifter, being an animal wasn't necessarily her strongest form.

"Hang on." Nix conjured two black jackets. She handed one off to Connor, who slipped it on over his pale blue shirt. Immediately, he blended in with the dark surroundings. She tugged on the other jacket, covering her pink T-shirt. I tugged my own jacket on.

Nix frowned. "Our faces are like beacons."

She had a point. We were pasty as Minnesotans in February.

Her magic swelled again, and she handed out a couple pots of dark gray powder. We smeared it on our faces.

"Hell camo," I said.

With our black clothes and the makeup, we blended well into the dark. Though Connor had brought enough invisibility potion for each of us, the stuff only lasted an hour. We had to save it for the castle.

We set off across the rocky black ground. There wasn't a single tree or bush to hide behind. The perfect place for a castle you meant to defend.

"This is like the surface of the moon," Connor said.

"But deadlier," I said.

We hiked in silence, everyone on high alert. Occasionally, the ground shifted beneath our feet, but no monsters popped up. I kept my ice magic charged and ready, though.

Something red glowed against the ground ahead, like thousands of gallons of glowing paint thrown across the landscape.

"What is that?" Roarke asked.

"Lava," Cade said. "But there's a path."

"And I bet it's a delightful stroll," Claire added.

I chuckled, but the laughter died as we neared. The heat was intense, the glow of the lava brilliant. I swallowed hard.

Cade pointed. "That way."

We followed his lead, going single file across a wide strip of stone. Lava bubbled on all sides. In the distance, there were little rock islands. All the movies I'd ever seen about people drowning in this stuff flashed in my mind. I was desperate to shift to my Phantom form, but I couldn't risk us being seen.

No one said a word as we raced across the bridge. Lava popped and bubbled beside us.

When we hit a magical barrier that prickled against my skin, the ground began to shift, cracking and separating. My heart leaped into my throat. Nix gasped.

"Shit." Connor jumped as the rock split ahead of us.

The ground underfoot broke up like an ice cap with a polar bear upon it. And that never went well for the polar bear. The stone that I stood upon tilted slightly. Sweat broke out on my skin, and my heart raced.

"Hang on," Roarke said.

Our winged companions took to the air, each picking up one of us as the ground broke. Even Cass shifted into a griffin, grabbing Nix. Roarke swooped me up, and Connor scrambled onto Aidan's broad back while Cade picked up Claire right before her slab of rock tilted into the lava.

I clung to Roarke as he flew us to the safety of the other side. Though 'safety' was relative. The heat rose, making sweat drip down my skin and my grip slippery on Roarke. Lava bubbled below. My stomach turned.

My heart was racing by the time he dropped me off. Once all my friends were standing on solid ground, I almost collapsed in relief.

But there was no time.

In the distance, a hoard of bats burst into the air, their wings fluttering in the night.

"What the hell?" Claire hissed. She hated bats.

Unfortunately for all of us, they weren't bats. As the figures neared, they grew larger.

Winged demons.

Strikingly familiar winged demons. They looked like Roarke and Cade, only with larger horns and uglier faces. Roarke's mom must have been really pretty. It was a stupid thought when fifty winged demons were charging.

"Shit!" Connor fumbled in his potion bag. "Time for invisibility."

I glanced around, but there was nowhere to run. Nowhere to hide. Though we'd hoped to save the stuff...

"Yeah, now's the time," I said.

Connor handed around the small vials. "Sniff before you drink. Should smell like oranges."

Oh crap. In the dark, he couldn't be sure which potions he was handing out.

I took mine and uncorked it. Immediately, I was hit by the scent of orange, so I chugged. It tasted like mud, but at this rate, I didn't care. Cass and Aidan shifted into their human forms and drank their potions.

Once everyone was invisible, we set off running. I used my stolen magic from the Whispa Demon to muffle the sound of our footsteps.

If only we could sneak past the demons...

For a little while, it worked. We could even see the castle on the horizon, growing closer and closer. It was pitch-black in color and seemed to be hazy—as if it, too, were made of shadows.

We just had to get there. Then we'd do our usual—sneak in and get the bad guy. Bad guys, plural, in this case.

I pushed myself harder, relying on my new magic to muffle the sounds of our footsteps and heavy breathing. The demons flew overhead, searching for us, but they had no luck. Apparently their sense of smell was terrible, or it'd been burned out by the acrid scent of this hellscape.

We were half a mile away when the air just ahead of us shimmered.

Shit.

Magical barrier.

I tried to pull to a halt, but it was too late. A shiver rippled over me. A demon shrieked, pointing to us.

"We're visible," Connor said.

"Oh, hell." I spun, looking up into the dark sky.

Fifty winged demons whirled to face us.

"I'll try illusion!" Cass cried. She'd stolen the power last summer and was well practiced with it. Hopefully she'd be able to conceal us from their eyes. Her magic swelled briefly on the air, but nothing happened. "Can't! It won't work."

"The barrier must block any kind of invisibility or stealth approach," I said.

"Shit," Aidan said. "That's complex magic for a place this big. These guys are *powerful* if they can pull that off."

He was right. We hadn't expected something *this* advanced.

That left us with outright warfare, if we wanted to survive.

The demons converged on us.

"We fight," Roarke said.

We'd agreed on it this morning. The Shadows needed me—but not my friends. Capture could mean death.

So fighting it was.

Already in their demon forms, Roarke and Cade took off into the air, their claws outstretched and snarls twisting their faces. Aidan shifted and followed, ready to rend flesh from bone.

Cass hurled a massive fireball at the demons. It collided with one, sending him flying ass over wings and straight into another demon.

Quickly, I shifted into my Phantom form, then threw an icicle at the nearest demon. It pierced him through the middle. Our winged friends protected Nix, Claire, Connor, and me as we hurled whatever weapons we had—arrows, potion bombs, icicles.

We did a damned good job, too, taking out nearly two dozen demons. But this was far more than we'd anticipated. Cade's recon hadn't suggested there would be fifty winged guards. But he was fighting as hard as

Roarke, blood pouring from claw wounds to his chest and back.

He hadn't betrayed us. We'd just gotten unlucky.

And unlucky in war sucked.

Sweat poured down my face as I hurled my icy weapons. The battle raged, bodies falling from the sky. Fortunately, they were all enemies who fell, but our side was struggling. Even in the dim light, I could see the blood pouring off Roarke, Aidan, and Cade.

Though my magic flagged from overuse, I kept going.

"I'm running low," Connor said. His potion bag was nearly empty.

"I can conjure more." Nix's magic swelled. "Nothing fancy. Acid bombs."

"It'll do."

Nix handed over the acid bombs, and Connor threw them, his accuracy incredible. He hit a demon from forty yards away. The acid bomb exploded, green and bright, and the demon shrieked.

We were close. There were only twenty demons left in the sky.

"We've got this!" I cried. Though how we were going to sneak in at this point, I had no idea. That was a problem for another time.

I charged up an icicle and sent it at the nearest demon. It plowed through his middle and then went through the demon behind. Nix fired her arrows, her aim deadly, while Connor and Claire continued to hurl acid bombs.

There were only five demons left in the sky when I caught sight of a figure floating across the ground toward us. A Shadow.

The dark power that emanated from him made me shudder. Before I could turn my attack toward him, he hurled a glowing yellow orb at us.

"Duck!" I yelled.

But it didn't matter. As soon as the orb hovered above us, it exploded, sending a magical sonic boom through the air that froze my muscles solid. Even the demons in the air froze, dropping like stones.

Horror rose as I watched Aidan, Roarke, and Cade plummet, then crash against the ground. No matter how I struggled, I couldn't break free.

We stood frozen for ages, until, finally, a small army of demons tromped across the horizon. There were probably about twenty of them, and they were all massive—at least seven feet tall. My heart thundered as I waited, my gaze racing around, trying to take stock of my friends. I thought everyone was mostly okay, though I couldn't tell.

When the demons arrived, they swept us up in their arms like planks of wood, hauling us across the moonlike ground and up to the black castle.

I'd never felt evil like what radiated from the structure looming ahead. It actually *was* made of shadows, but also black stone. Turrets and towers rose high into the gray sky. Black mist hovered around the structure. It was like a fairytale castle warped and twisted by evil.

As they carried us through the massive gate, I tried to reach out for my friends. But I couldn't. I was so stiff and solid I wondered if I'd ever move again.

I screamed inside as they carried my friends away from me, toward another part of the castle. Cade had described this place as best he could, though he'd only visited a few rooms.

He'd never been to a dungeon, but I prayed that's where they were going. Anywhere except to the executioner.

I strained to take in everything around me as the big demon hauled me across the courtyard and up a massive flight of stairs. Even inside, everything was dark. The light that glimmered from wall sconces was almost gray. It was all as Cade had described it, though he hadn't managed to convey the sense of hopelessness that welled over a person when they entered a place like this.

Instead of a dungeon, they took me to a library.

It was horrible.

I'd thought I could love any library.

I'd been *so* wrong. Every book in there was bound in tar-black leather. I'd have put big money down in Vegas that these books were bound in human and demon skin. Whatever secrets they contained, I didn't want to know.

The demon tossed me on the ground in front of a fireplace that flickered with black flame. Immediately, a Shadow swept into the room. It was dressed in the usual black cloak that shimmered at the edges.

The demon bowed low, then slipped out of the library.

The sudden silence was oppressive. It took everything I had to calm my raging mind and focus on my surroundings. Now was *not* the time to freak out.

One thing was immediately clear.

This wasn't the Shadow who had cursed Cade, and therefore, me. Cade had said I'd be able to feel it. I felt nothing but pure evil from this one as it drifted over to hover in front of me. When it waved a shadowy hand, the magic that bound me disappeared.

Immediately, my muscles ached. I rolled to my feet, drawing my sword from the ether.

The Shadow thrust out his right hand, palm toward me. I slammed back into a big wooden chair. No matter how I strained, I couldn't escape.

"Body control?" I choked out.

He inclined his head.

The other Shadow that I'd fought had been able to whip out parts of his shadowy form like octopus tentacles. But they all appeared to have different talents.

Inside, I screamed for Draka.

I got nothing.

"So good of you to join us." The voice was low and silky. The fact that it was a pleasant tone was somehow worse.

I glanced around and tried to subtly suck in a stabilizing breath. "Don't you think this place is a bit overdone? I mean, I get that you're called the Shadows and all, but this is a bit much."

"I have no interest in your jokes."

"I've got nothing but time, considering I can't move." I had no idea if heckling him was a good idea, but I wanted to throw him off his guard.

Perhaps I could call for Pond Flower as a distraction. But she wasn't a fraction as strong as Draka. I hated to bring her into this while I was frozen, unable to help her.

"You once wanted to be part of this." The Shadow's words threw me for a loop. "You will want to be part of it again."

"What?"

"Watch." He waved his arm in front of him. An image appeared.

My parents sat on a couch, with me sitting on a small cushion at their feet. A fire flickered in the hearth at my back and a tea set sat on the ornate table at our side. It was the single most homey scene I'd ever seen with them. My heart twisted in my chest.

I was young in this scene—it must have taken place before they'd given me to the Monster.

"You will open the portal, Delphine." My mother's voice resonated with power. Though the scene was homey, her tone was not.

"How, Mother?" The excitement in my young voice made me wince.

"It is your fated gift. You know that we are World Walkers, able to cross from hell to Earth. But *you*. You are the strongest of them all. When you have mastered your power, you will be able to tear down the barrier between the Underworld and Earth."

"The *whole* barrier?" My eyes gleamed with excitement.

How could I like the idea of that? Even as a child? Not to mention—*holy shit*. My mysterious superpower was basically destroying the world?

Ugh. That sucked.

"You are the only one who can do it. You will create a portal large enough to transport all the demons to Earth. They won't need an Earth-bound supernatural to help them, and no additional magic. They will be free to cross."

"And I'll save them." Pride rang in my voice.

Cunning entered my mother's eyes. She smiled grimly.

"Yes, you will save them all. The demons who suffer so badly will be freed upon the earth." My mother smiled benignly. "And the horrible humans will be ended. Their evil and cruelty will be gone from the world. You will be their Demise."

Nausea twisted my gut. *That* was how she'd done it. Spun a story that was wholly opposite of the truth.

My mother was clever, and I had been young.

Out of the corner of my eye, I caught sight of the Shadow beside me. Watching me. He fiddled with something in his hand, then magic shimmered around him, something new. A white haze that crept toward me. But my mother spoke again, distracting me.

"You will practice hard?" Desperation glinted in her eyes.

My younger self nodded eagerly.

I found myself agreeing with her. Of course I would practice hard. I had to save the demons and be the demise of the humans. The world needed me. That terrible barrier had to come down.

I shook my head, confusion clouding my mind.

Had I really just thought that I needed to tear down the barrier and release the demons onto the earth? That was freaking nuts.

From beside me, the Shadow's wispy magic reached out toward me. When I breathed, I tasted the mist on my tongue. Cloves. It tasted like cloves.

Holy fates. He was using some kind of magic to control my mind. In addition to the Influenta Curse, it was an extra layer of control—they were *serious* about making me do their bidding.

Which meant they were worried I'd fight the Influenta Curse. That meant I *could* fight it. Hope flared. They were scared of my free will, so they were trying to crush it.

I closed my eyes, sucking in a deep breath and trying to resist. I focused on my goal. On my friends. But my eyes snapped open against my will, forced to watch.

Over and over again, the scene played in front of me as I struggled to fight the Shadow's control. He was forcing me to watch—to return to that mindset. When I was that young, I'd have done anything to please my parents.

It took everything I had to protect a scrap of my mind. I prayed it was enough, because no matter how hard I tried, I kept falling back into the Shadow's magic, believing that I really should help destroy the barrier between the Underworld and Earth. I was the only one who could do it. If I didn't do it, who would?

Finally, the scene in front of me ceased. I blinked, slowly coming back to myself. But I wasn't fully myself, not really.

The Shadow's magic still hung heavily over my mind. I fought it, keeping it at bay, but it was still there. Still lurking.

"Do you see? You want to be part of this," the Shadow said.

I turned to him. "Yes, you're right." My speech was slow.

He smiled, nodding in a satisfied manner.

And honestly, I couldn't blame him.

Because I *did* kind of believe that I wanted to help. My mind flashed back and forth between myself in the present and myself in the past. So when I told him that I wanted to help, part of me meant it.

Inwardly, I shook myself. I shouldn't be falling for this!

I focused on the thought of my friends, trapped somewhere deep inside this castle. They needed me. I had to remember them. They'd keep me grounded.

"Then rise," the Shadow said. "We will prepare the chamber."

Slowly, I stood. "The chamber?"

"We did not know when you would come to us, so there are things to be done." He snapped his fingers, and two demons appeared in the room. They were massive beasts at least eight feet tall with huge horns and hands that could tear me apart.

They were easily the scariest demons I had ever seen.

"These will be your companions while you wait," the Shadow said.

Companions. I almost scoffed, but just managed to hold it in. I didn't want him knowing I wasn't one hundred percent into his plan.

And the horrible truth was, occasionally, I'd think to myself that the plan wasn't actually so bad. When thoughts of my friends wouldn't ground me, I'd reach for the bracelet that Roarke had given me, rubbing my fingers against it.

The demons led me down a wide corridor, one at my front and one at my back. I saw no one as we walked. I felt a presence, though. Black mist hovered in front of the stone. Were the Shadows part of the castle?

I shuddered.

Nah. That was too crazy.

But still, I studied the stone as I walked, looking for eyes.

This whole place was getting to me.

The demons led me up a tall spiral staircase to a chamber at the top of the tower. Memories of my childhood flashed in my mind. This wasn't the same place, but I *hated* towers now.

There was nothing in the room—not even a chair. No windows, either, so throwing myself out wasn't an option. I stood awkwardly in the middle of the room while the demons each stood beside the door.

Hmmm.

I needed a plan. Because hanging out in here, waiting for my own shit to get really dire, was not going to work.

CHAPTER FOURTEEN

My mind raced at I collected and discarded plans. I tried calling upon my ice magic. If I could just send a bolt through each of their chests, I'd be golden.

Of course, my ice magic lay dormant inside me. In fairness, this would be a terrible holding cell if it allowed me to use violent magic.

Which meant I had to get out of here, *then* use violent magic.

Tentatively, I tried my Phantom form, doing my best to only turn part of my body Phantom. I didn't want the guards getting even a hint of my plan. When my fingertips glowed blue, I grinned. I tried pulling my sword from the ether, but it didn't come.

Damn.

Though not surprising. A sword definitely counted as violent magic. At least I could adopt my Phantom form. It wouldn't do me much good in a fight against these guys, but fortunately, I didn't want it for a fight.

I retreated inside my mind, trying to remember the spiral staircase that had led up to this tower. It was directly below this room, filling the bottom portion of the tower. If the door was directly across from me, then that meant there was an open space leading onto the stairs right below me. I shifted left a couple feet for good measure.

"Don't move," growled one of the guards.

This plan was nuts, but it was all I had. Not wanting to alert the guards, I prayed for luck rather than knocking on my head.

I called upon my Phantom form, shifting as quickly as I could. Then I jumped up, willing myself to sink through the floor when I landed. I rarely used this trick, but when I fell through to the stairs directly below the room, I grinned.

Then almost shrieked and stumbled backward.

Another massive demon waited on the stairs, blocking my escape.

The Shadows had been prepared for anything.

My heart leaped into my throat as I called on my ice magic, praying that the protective enchantments on the room above didn't extend to down here.

Fortunately, my magic swelled within me. When I heard the demons from the room above open the door, I called for Pond Flower. I didn't stand a chance alone. One demon blocked my way down, and two more were coming from above.

I felt Pond Flower as soon as she appeared on the steps above me, but didn't turn to look. The demon below was charging toward me, massive hands reaching out. I powered up an icicle and sent it straight through his chest.

It pierced him, sending him reeling, then toppling down the stairs. *Shit!* I didn't want him rolling out into the corridor at the bottom and being seen.

I threw my ice magic outward, creating a thick wall in the stairwell. The demon's body slammed into it, stopping abruptly.

I turned, just in time to see a demon trip over Pond Flower, who blocked their way. He hurtled down, passing through my Phantom form and slamming into the ice wall that I'd created.

The last demon stopped right before Pond Flower. She growled, her black flame rising up from her fur. The protective barrier.

Thank you, Pond Flower.

The demon edged down toward her, his eyes bright with violence, then pulled up short. He couldn't get close lest he risk her horrible flame.

So he risked my ice instead. Just as he hurled a blade at me, I sent an icicle through his chest. His silver blade flew end over end. I dodged, though not quickly enough. It sliced across my shoulder. Pain blossomed in my arm.

Fortunately, my icicle hit my target, sinking deep into his chest. His eyes widened, and he clutched the wound. I glanced at my own wound, grateful to see that it wasn't terribly long or deep. My leather jacket had helped protect me.

Hoping that the demon was done for, I whirled and raced after the one who'd fallen down the stairs. He was struggling to his feet, one leg clearly broken.

A tinge of guilt streaked through me. Though he was massive and huge and in the employ of someone evil, I hated attacking someone injured.

But my friends… If I didn't get out of here and save them, they'd be dead.

I sucked in a breath and sent an icicle through the chest of the last demon. The demon fell, bleeding out on the stairs.

I considered taking at least one of their powers, but I didn't have time. Who knew what could be happening to my friends right now.

Pond Flower and I skirted around him, slipping through the ice wall. I walked through in my Phantom form. She just disappeared on one side and reappeared on the other.

"Thanks for coming," I whispered. "That trip maneuver saved my butt."

She smiled up at me, tongue lolling. It was easier to hang on to rational thought while she was with me—she grounded me. Though the Shadows' magic was still inside my mind, making me think that maybe it wasn't the *worst* idea to help them break the barrier between the Underworld and Earth, Pond Flower reminded me of who I was and what was really important.

We hurried down the stairs, stopping abruptly when we reached the corridor.

A Shadow stood, blocking our way.

The hair at my nape stood on end. Immediately, I could feel that he wasn't the one who had cursed Cade and me. Though he had no face that I could see beneath his ephemeral black cloak, surprise rolled off of him.

I wasted no time calling my sword from the ether and lunging. It was the only way to kill a Shadow that I had found. Before my blade could make contact with his form, his hand whipped out.

Electricity shot through me, pain like I'd never felt. I faltered, nearly dropping my blade. The Shadow hit me again. I smelled burning.

My hair?

Shit, this was going to hell fast.

I gripped my sword and pushed through the pain, lunging for him. He danced back, too quick, and hit me with another bolt of electricity.

I fell to my knees, vision blurring.

From the corner of my eye, I saw Pond Flower creeping around behind the Shadow. She'd turned fully to black flame, and her eyes glowed bright red. She was one scary bitch.

She crept up behind the Shadow, clearly intent on pulling a tripping maneuver like last time. Fortunately, the Shadow's gaze was on me. I could feel him charging up his electricity. He was about to strike.

All I had to do was muster one last drop of energy and get my blade through him. A moment later, Pond Flower was right behind him. I lunged to my feet, striking out with my blade. The Shadow leaped back, tripping over Pond Flower.

I followed, piercing him through the chest with my sword. I felt the strangest sensation as he fell back, slipping off the blade.

Though he lashed out with his electricity again, it was weak. I'd landed a mortal blow.

His cloak fluttered as he fell, a shadowy apparition that was both real and not quite. Instinctually, I reached out and grabbed the edge of it. I yanked hard, pulling it off of him.

It came easily, fluttering toward me. The Shadow itself was roughly human shaped, though I still couldn't make out features. Though I'd called them men in my head, there was no gender that I could determine.

The body faded quickly into the stone below.

Becoming one with the castle?

I prayed it was really dead.

The cloak hung limply from my hand. It felt like silk and smoke, a strange combination that was imbued with dark magic and evil.

I shuddered as I pulled it on. Pond Flower stepped back briefly, concern in her red eyes and her fur on end.

"It's okay," I whispered. "Just a disguise."

She padded up, sniffing me. Her fur flattened, relaxing. Though I couldn't blame her for being freaked out. Wearing this thing felt awful. Like a slimy touch that was also prickly. It even made it harder for me to remember what my real goal was. Save my friends or help the Shadows?

No matter how hard I tried with my stolen demon magic, I couldn't fully overcome the magic that I'd inhaled.

I reached out, sinking my fingertips into Pond Flower's fur, seeking her grounding presence. The black flame that encompassed her in her full-on hellhound form tickled my fingers. It'd kill anyone else, but our strange connection made it pleasant for me. When she looked like this, with her brown and white spots fully consumed by the black flame, she nearly blended into the strange castle walls.

"Stay like this," I whispered. "You're hidden. Stick close to the wall."

An ornate silver mirror hung on the wall across from me. Even I nearly blended into the castle wall. When I pulled the hood up, it was hard to tell I wasn't a Shadow.

"Two goals," I whispered to Pond Flower. I felt more myself when I was talking. "Kill the Shadow who cursed Cade and me, then rescue my friends."

I called upon my dragon sense, using it to find both my friends and the Shadow that I sought. By my calculations, there should be four Shadows left. I'd slain one back in Germany and then one right now— hopefully. I prayed that the other four weren't all clustered together. I could really only handle one at a time.

Fortunately, my friends and the Shadow were all on the bottom floor of the castle. In the dungeons, probably.

Pond Flower and I crept along, our footsteps silent on the stone beneath our feet. The whole castle vibrated with dark magic, and the walls never stopped looking weird. Almost like the castle was built of smoke, but not. One strong wind could blast it away.

My dragon sense tugged us through dark corridors and by massive rooms. But there was very little furniture. If there was a barracks for the demons, maybe that would show signs of life, but I didn't think the Shadows were truly alive. They were more like sentient evil.

I shuddered, following my dragon sense to a stairwell that led down. This, too, was a spiral staircase. I tugged the cloak tighter about myself, hoping to pass as a Shadow if I came across any demons. I kept my ice magic charged up, just in case.

The staircase led down at least four flights, and it got hotter with every step. By the time I reached the bottom, I was sweating. The hallway was wider here, with doorways positioned all the way down.

Why were the Shadows down here? Were they threatening my friends? I hurried, muffling my footsteps with my sound magic.

Soon, my dragon sense was going off like mad, tugging hard to the doorway on the left. I sidled up to it, holding my breath. When I peeked in, I got a glimpse of three Shadows, all standing around a table and looking at a piece of paper.

I jerked back and squeezed my eyes shut.

Shit.

I couldn't take three. I'd be killed, then my friends would rot in the dungeons. Or worse. Even just looking at the Shadows made me think that maybe I should go in and join them. Help them with their plan.

Damn the magic that had twisted my mind.

Quietly, I sucked in a deep breath, getting a hold of my mind. Pond Flower pressed herself against my legs, making it easier.

Fortunately, none of the Shadows had been facing the door, so I was able to slip by without them noticing. The corridor turned right about twenty yards later. The air began to stink—that awful dungeon smell that was so characteristic of places like this. Blood, bowels, fear.

I prayed that my friends were okay as Pond Flower and I slipped along. Every now and again I'd sink my hands into her fur to remind myself of my goals. This mind control stuff sucked.

My dragon sense pulled hard as I reached the end of the hall. I was so close—I could feel them. Just on the other side of the heavy door.

Footsteps sounded behind me.

Shit.

I glanced around, spotting an open door. I ducked in, Pond Flower behind me.

Of course it was too good to be true. Whoever was stomping their way down the hall turned into the room. I had a half second to check out the back of the demon. I used it, sending an icicle into his back before he could turn around. He grunted then fell.

When no one else came in, I sagged against the wall, panting.

That had been close.

I gave it a few more seconds, then peered out into the hall. No one was there, so I hurried out, headed straight for the door to the dungeons. I'd just drift right through in my Phantom form and—

Yelping sounded from behind me. I spun, shock and fear hitting me like a baseball bat to the head.

One of the Shadows had Pond Flower. Somehow, he'd gotten ahold of her with his shadowy arms. And it hurt her. The yelps were growing louder and louder.

Two more Shadows drifted beside the one holding Pond Flower. She wouldn't leave because I was still here.

"Go, Pond Flower!" I screamed.

She struggled, trying to break free to get to me. But I knew she could use her magic to disappear back to the FireSoul headquarters.

She refused to.

"Go!" I put every ounce of command that I possessed into the word.

Her eyes rolled, then she disappeared. I prayed she went back to the FireSoul hideout.

Inside, I screamed for Draka, but I knew it wouldn't work. She'd never come when I called—only when my life was truly threatened. And even then, she didn't always show.

I drew my sword. But as soon as I took a step forward, I pulled up short, slamming into an invisible wall.

What the hell?

"You won't hurt us." The Phantom's voice sent a shiver through me. It was as deep as the ocean and as powerful as the moon pulling the tides.

This was the Shadow who had cursed Cade, and therefore, me.

Shit.

I lowered the sword as my mind screamed to fight. As my body fought my mind, it was the most horrible sensation in the world—like the molecules in my body were tearing apart from each other. But this Shadow controlled me as surely as he'd controlled Cade.

"Remove the cloak." His voice resonated with power.

Against my own volition, I reached up and removed the wispy cloak. Despite these awful circumstances, it felt good when the thing finally slipped off.

"Come with us." The Shadow turned and walked away. The others followed.

No matter how hard I tried to resist, I couldn't. My feet kept walking. It took all my strength, but I managed to turn my head, gazing back at the dungeons. I could only do it because he hadn't commanded me not to.

Pond Flower appeared out of thin air, standing right in front of the heavy wooden door. She looked skinnier than she had—as if the Shadow had sucked some of the life from her—but her eyes burned bright.

She took a step toward me, but I begged her not to, using only my eyes and my will. She couldn't fight the Shadows.

But she could possibly help my friends.

Save them, I begged. *Save them.*

If all I managed was to deliver Pond Flower to them, maybe it would be enough. After all, they had some serious magic themselves. With her help, they could escape.

They had to. Because there was nothing I could do now.

Pond Flower hesitated, then nodded, her eyes flaring red as black flame ignited along her fur. I wasn't fully sure what kind of magic hellhounds possessed, but I hoped it was enough.

The Shadows forced me to follow them to a massive room on the ground floor of the castle. Every step was painful, my mind fighting my body every inch of the way. But no matter how hard I tried, I couldn't break free. When we finally arrived, I was grateful to stop.

The room was round and high ceilinged—almost as big as an indoor football stadium. I'd known this place was big, but this was incredible.

As I stepped into the huge space, my gaze caught on the contraption in the middle. Confusion flared. It was a massive machine, some kind of intricate bronze device that was two stories high with a central platform. Arms spread out from it, like some weird, upturned spider.

"What the hell is that?" I blurted. Apparently, the Shadow hadn't controlled my tongue.

"You truly know nothing." The Shadow who controlled me turned. I considered him the lead Shadow, though I wasn't sure if that were true. "You have been the single greatest disappointment of this entire endeavor."

The true disappointment in his tone forced a laugh from me. "Eh, I can't say that's too upsetting for me."

But what the hell was going on? Was this the big shebang? Did this contraption have anything to do with me tearing a hole in the ether? The machine looked like some kind of crazy steampunk contraption—I'd never seen anything even remotely like it outside of Sci-Fi.

Whatever it was, I wanted nothing to do with it. I struggled against my bonds, but was unable to so much as move an inch.

"What is that thing?" I demanded again.

The Shadow who controlled me drifted around the machine, his bearing that of a proud father.

"When your parents failed to help you learn your magic, we realized we needed another way to convince you."

I couldn't see his frown, but I could *feel* it.

"Though you were enthusiastic as a child, you resisted later in life. You've never come into your magic because your subconscious refuses."

"Refuses? Yeah, maybe that's because I don't want to tear down the barrier between the Underworld and Earth—ever think of that? Why would I want my superpower to be causing the end of the world?" It really was a shit superpower. Cass had gotten infinite magic. I was the grim reaper.

"It wouldn't be the end of the world."

I laughed. "Demons are in hell for a reason. That's their *home*. The only reason they want to come to Earth is to feed on humans and other supernaturals' power."

The Shadow shrugged. "Yes."

"That's it? Yes?"

"Yes. The demons want that. We are here to fulfill that." He gestured to the machine. "And this will help."

"How?"

"When you refused to come into your magic, we realized that we needed something that would force you to do so. Though I can control your will, forcing you to dredge up magic that is deep inside you is beyond my capability. You've never been able to do it on your own, so I can't force you into it. It is the reason we did not seek you sooner. We needed this machine."

Huh. I'd wondered about that.

"It is an ancient device, meant to enhance a supernatural's magic. It will trigger your power, forcing you to create the portal that will destroy the barrier between the Underworld and Earth."

I flinched. If that were possible…

"You were meant to be our queen." True disappointment rang in his voice. These guys really had been expecting a lot from me. "We'd hoped to convince you. If you'd embraced your role, you would be. You could be useful to this cause. But as long as you fight us, it is too difficult. So you will become a tool. Create the portal, then you will be discarded."

Screw that.

When one of the Shadows had told me I'd be queen, part of me had liked that. Who didn't want to be queen?

But queen of *this*?

Nope.

"You can just go f—"

"Shut up."

My mouth snapped shut. Apparently he *could* control my ability to speak.

"Now turn back time. There." He pointed to the machine. "Take the machine back three thousand years."

Three thousand years? This thing was that old? Why did I have to take it back?

"Do it!"

The command jumpstarted my magic. I called it up from within myself. Agony tore through my chest as I fought the urge, but I couldn't stop it. I'd practiced this power enough that it came naturally. My time-turning magic flowed through me, impossible to stop.

Draka! I screamed in my mind as the blue glow of my magic spread out across the floor, traveling to the machine. I tried to turn time back only a hundred years, hoping that the modification would go unnoticed.

It felt like something stabbed me in the chest. Only after I'd glanced down did I realize I wasn't actually bleeding.

"Do not deviate," the Shadow commanded.

My magic pushed farther, fully encompassing the machine. The whole thing glowed blue as the clock was turned back.

Slowly, gems began to appear at each arm of the machine. Then something began to shimmer into existence on top of the portal. It was a rough lump of black stone. So simple and plain, but somehow more impressive for it.

Magic surged from the gems and the rock. These were the fuel for the machine. No wonder they had gone missing sometime in the machine's past. Stolen, probably.

With the gems in place, the brass arms began to whirl, spinning slowly, then faster and faster. They whipped up a breeze that blew my hair back from my face. The lump of rock at the center glowed brightly, almost blinding.

My time-turning magic faded as the machine whirled, silent except for the rush of wind. The four Shadows stood, staring in awe.

Did I have a moment to stop this?

I tried pulling on my magic, drawing it back into myself so that the machine turned to the present and its magical batteries faded.

Nothing happened. The thing had taken on a life of its own.

I swallowed hard, pushing my magic desperately. I had to stop this!

As the whole machine began to glow white with magic, something warmed inside me. An electric current of magic shot up from the central pillar on the machine and lashed toward me, striking me in the chest.

I stiffened, unable to control my body as power shot through me like an electric current. Light blared in front of my eyes, and I realized that it was coming from *me*.

Power vibrated along my skin, an unfamiliar warmth that filled me with light and strength and magic and every good thing I could ever imagine.

I was invincible.

I was power incarnate.

No! Something tugged at my mind.

The memory of taking power from the demons— how I hadn't wanted to once upon a time, in case there were dangerous side effects.

This was the epitome of a dangerous side effect.

I was becoming a monster.

I was becoming the Demise.

It had all started, and I had *failed* to stop it.

Aethelred had been right.

Tears poured down my cheeks as I stood there, unable to move or stop the magic that flowed through me.

"Create the portal!" the Shadow yelled.

No! I screamed it in my mind because my lips were welded shut by his magic.

"Create the portal!"

I fought his command, but my magic didn't. It felt like it linked with the contraption, then spread outward. I could feel the ether like a living thing. Like it was water full of bubbles that I could move at my will.

On the far wall, the air began to shimmer until it truly looked like glittering silver bubbles—like the tiny ones in champagne.

I fought the Shadow's command, desperate to stop their horrible plan.

But the bubbles parted in the air, separating to reveal a jagged scar in the ether. Just like the first time I'd torn my way out of the Underworld when I'd come back to life.

What a dark power I possessed.

The tear widened, growing to the size of a small car. I fought it, knowing that somehow it was I who created this hole. It couldn't get any bigger!

My muscles trembled with the strain, and my vision blurred. Sweat poured down my face.

Finally, I collapsed. I didn't even feel the stone ground as I fell.

"No!" a Shadow shouted.

Through blurry vision, I could see him lunge toward me.

The lead Shadow stopped his companion. "Wait. We will test it."

Oriamor? I squinted, trying to make out what was through the portal. My vision cleared, but the scene through the portal did not. It was gray. Hazy.

The Shadow whistled low. Three demons entered. He flicked a hand toward the first, a hulking beast with pale gray skin. "Walk through."

The demon frowned, but approached the blurry portal. He hesitated briefly, then stepped through it. His form took a few seconds to sink through—as if the portal were made of pudding—but soon, he'd disappeared.

My insides twisted with pain. Tears leaked down my cheeks. *I'd failed.* That demon had walked through to earth.

"It worked," one of the Shadows whispered in awe.

"Next," the Shadow said.

The second demon approached the portal, attempting to step through. It took several minutes, everyone one of which was torture, but he made it through. I could do nothing but lay there and watch as strength slowly returned to my limbs.

I'd done this.

"It's magnificent," the lead Shadow said.

"It is slow, though," said another.

"It is weak because she resisted us, but it will strengthen. It has the magic necessary to let a demon through without any additional magic. Soon, they will flow through to Oriamor. One after the other without cease."

"How long until it is complete?" the Shadow demanded.

The lead Shadow said, "It will grow stronger with every moment, allowing demons to pass more quickly. In days, the demons will be able to stream through. Sixty per minute. Maybe more. *We* will be able to walk through. The magic produced by the machine will speed it up. We don't need her anymore."

Shit.

"Finally," breathed a Shadow. "Finally, it has worked."

They stood in awe, staring at the portal. The machine continued to whirl, magical energy filling the air. It gave me strength. Already, my muscles were feeling better. My mind, too.

I had to use this. While the Shadows were in awe of their evil creation, I had to rescue my friends. Then we could stop this. Somehow.

Unfortunately, we were on the bottom floor of the castle. There was only ground below me. Though I wished for a dungeon below, somehow I knew there wasn't. My Phantom senses shuddered at the idea of sinking through the floor like I'd done in the tower, the same way I'd shudder at the idea of stepping off a cliff.

Death waited that way.

I'd probably come back, but far too late.

I had to crawl. The door was only thirty feet away, in the opposite direction of the Shadows. Silently, using my new control over sound, I crept toward the door.

I was almost there when I heard a shout.

One of the Shadows had turned and spotted me.

Shit.

The lead Shadow swept around, coming to stand between me and the exit. Escape slipped through my fingers. I wanted to scream.

The malevolence in his demeanor sent a shiver through me. They no longer needed me.

"Stop!" Magic swelled around the Shadow.

I tried to move, to run, but he'd frozen me in place. Terror beat its fists against my ribs.

He was about to strike—I had no idea with what kind of magic—when I heard the most glorious sound ever…

Hellhound toenails clicked on stone, somewhere in the hallway. I glanced toward the door. Pond Flower hurtled into the room, her eyes lit with red flame and her fur with black. Behind her, my friends charged in, every one of them.

Nix and Cass gave harsh battle cries.

The Shadow who controlled me whirled.

It was my only chance. He'd let go of his command of me, though only for a moment. I leaped up, adopting my Phantom form and drawing my sword from the ether. I lunged for his back, sinking my blade deep.

He shrieked, a horrible sound that made my ears ache, and collapsed to his knees. Before he could utter a word, I yanked my blade free and swung at his neck, taking his head in a clean blow.

My faded blue glow turned brilliant again. The curse was lifted.

"Demons!" a Shadow yelled from behind.

Calling for backup.

Roarke, Aidan, and Cade transformed and took to the air, their powerful wings carrying them high. As my other friends surged into the room, they hurled their weapons. Flame, acid bombs, arrows—all meant for the Shadows. But nothing struck.

Only I could kill the Shadows. And there were three more.

Demons surged into the room, an endless line.

"Stop the machine!" I cried.

From what the Shadow had said, it sped up the portal. It needed to be stopped.

My winged friends flew for it, attempting to stop the whirling arms or to steal the lump of stone from the middle. The Shadows rushed toward the portal. To protect it?

Cass and Nix joined me, along with Claire and Connor. In seconds, we set up our usual battle station—back to back with a wall of heavy sandbags provided by Nix. The stuff was surprisingly good at blocking magic.

"How'd you get out?" I cried as I hurtled an icicle at a massive demon who charged us. There had to be over thirty in the room now. What the hell should I attack first? Demons, Shadows, machine?

If we could take the demons out, we could deal with the machine and the Shadows, who still hovered by the portal, chanting some kind of spell.

I needed to get to them.

"We were in an enchanted sleep." Cass threw a fireball the size of a Buick at a group of demons. "Pond Flower woke us. Hellhound breath. You know how it is."

Pond Flower, her fur alight with her protective black flame, prowled circles around our sandbag defenses, growling deep in her throat. The demons couldn't touch her, not like the Shadows could, and her magic repelled them, providing us with an extra level of protection.

I took out two demons with the same icicle, about to jump over the barrier and head for the Shadows.

But demons continued to flow into the room. More and more of them. We'd been fighting for only about twenty seconds, and already we were outnumbered. Winged ones arrived, too, attacking Roarke, Aidan, and Cade as they flew around the machine.

"We aren't going to beat the demons." I turned my attention to the machine. "There are too many."

"Yeah," Nix said.

"You guys need to run for it," I said. "Cass, transport everyone out of here."

"I hate to leave a fight." Cass hurled a fireball.

"Better to live and fight another day." Because we *would* die here. There were far too many demons. They'd beaten us outside the castle and they'd beat us here. I'd never reach the portal to try to shut it—if I could even figure out how. Worse, the machine would continue to spin, and the portal continue to grow.

"Amen to that," Cass said.

"Take them." I nodded to Claire and Connor, who threw potion bombs with deadly accuracy.

"You're not staying here," Cass shouted.

"I'm coming."

"You're planning something." Cass shot me a knowing look.

"I've got to destroy that machine." It was the only thing that I knew could help. Roarke and the others were having no luck, especially now that the winged demons were here.

No matter what, the machine had to go first. I couldn't fight three Shadows at once without certain death—but I could destroy this source of horrible magic and slow the portal.

I jumped over the barrier, racing to the machine. I got as close to the base as I could, kneeling down to press my hands to the stone floor. As I fed my ice magic into the ground, sending it straight to the machine, demons converged on me.

Roarke flew down, followed by Aidan, and they managed to hold off some of the demons as I forced my magic toward the machine. But with winged demons attacking from the air, my guardians were flagging.

My ice magic had only raced partway up the machine, and even that part wasn't yet frozen. Above me, Roarke and Aidan grappled with the demons. More flew toward me.

I was going to run out of time!

With no one to watch my back while I did this, I'd never make it.

A beautiful shriek filled the air. My heart leaped as my gaze darted to the door. There was nothing there.

But that *had* to be Draka's cry.

The ceiling exploded, debris flying everywhere. Draka, her blue glow brilliant in the dark room, swooped in, followed by her three Phantom dragon brethren. The ones I'd met in the cave.

Instead of attacking the demons, the Phantom dragons landed near me, encircling me in the protective shield of their wings. My world glowed brilliant blue as I forced my ice magic toward the machine.

With the Phantom dragons protecting me, my magic flowed quickly. They may have even lent me some of their power. Through a gap in their wings, I could see ice begin to form on the gleaming brass.

I fed it more magic, having to compensate for the heat caused by the friction of the whirling apparatus. Within moments, it creaked to a halt.

Finally, Roarke was able to get near. He swooped over top of the machine and plucked the stone from the platform.

With the source of its magic gone, the metal grew dim beneath the coating of ice. I called upon my new gift of telekinesis, commanding the roof debris to hurl itself at the machine. Stone and tile hurtled through the air, colliding with the machine like gunfire. The metal was so cold and the blows so powerful that it shattered, raining down upon the ground.

The Shadows shrieked, their rage palpable.

Before I could blink, Draka plucked me from the ground and carried me high into the air.

The scene in the room below made my stomach drop.

Every inch of the floor was covered with demons. Even the space where my friends had set up their battle stations was overrun by the bastards.

I prayed they'd made it out.

I didn't have time to search as Draka burst through the hole in the roof and out into the sky. The last thing I saw were the three Shadows staring up at me, rage vibrating around them like a living thing.

"Del!" Roarke's voice carried across the night.

I twisted in Draka's grip, catching sight of him, Aidan, and Cade, who'd all flown out with us. Relief surged through me, weakening my muscles. If they were here, that meant the others had transported out. They'd never have left them behind, and Pond Flower could transport herself out whenever she pleased. Roarke even had the magical lump of stone trapped in his arms.

The relief was short-lived.

The ground below teemed with demons.

Thousands. They were like ants surging over rotten food.

We'd never be able to return here to fight. And soon, all of these demons would flow through the portal onto earth.

I'd failed.

So badly.

Live to fight another day. Draka's voice was clear in my head. As if she could read my thoughts and my despair. *We must leave. Tell your friends to join my brethren. We must escape this land immediately.*

She was right. There was no victory for us here. Not now. Our only hope was the future. And to have that, we had to escape.

"Guys! Ride a dragon. They'll get us out of here!"

They did as I asked, and quickly. When I heard the wings beating behind us, I turned. More of the winged demons were after us. We really did have to get out of here soon.

Draka shot toward the sky, so fast that the wind blinded me. A second later, the ether sucked me in.

CHAPTER FIFTEEN

The Next Day

With Draka at my side, I stood in the underground throne room at my parents' castle in Wales, forcing my new magic into the portal that the Shadows had used to release demons into this room two weeks ago.

After tending to our battle wounds, we'd caught a few hours sleep, then come here immediately. First, we'd set out feelers for Oriamor, sending messages to every contact we had to try to locate the place. In the meantime, the first thing I needed to do was practice my portal magic.

Fortunately, I had a portal to practice on.

As expected, this portal led into another part of their deserted wasteland of an Underworld. It was a very small one, and the type that could only transport a few demons if they had the right kind of Earthbound supernatural sponsor to help them cross. But I was going to try to get rid of it.

If my horrible new magic could create tears in the ether, surely it could mend them?

With demons currently flowing out of the mysterious Oriamor portal, I needed to learn this skill.

"Keep going." Draka's voice sounded distant, though she was right next to me in her human form.

Sweat rolled down my temple as I fed my unfamiliar magic into the ether, envisioning stitching up the tear as if it were a torn sweater. Warmth glowed in my chest as the magic surged.

Finally, the ether began to mend. Hope flared in my chest. If I could master this, then I could close the portal I'd created.

My magic began to wane, growing weaker as I used it up. I pushed harder, giving it everything I had. But the portal remained half open. My head grew woozy as I tried. Mind spinning, I swayed.

Draka's hand touched my shoulder. "That is enough for now."

"No," I rasped.

"Stop." She squeezed lightly.

About to tip over, I pulled back on my magic, despair filling my chest like black tar. "I failed."

"No." Draka's voice was hard. "You didn't. You've closed half the portal. You *can* do this. You just need practice."

"Practice takes time. We don't have time."

"We don't have a plan either," Draka said. "You wanted to rush here and try this. Now that you've proven you can do it, it is time to plan."

Draka was right. I turned to face my friends, who had all insisted on coming along. Partially because we'd been afraid there might actually be demons here and I'd need the backup, but also because we hadn't had a chance to discuss the future.

Even Pond Flower had come. Apparently yesterday had been too close for comfort, and she hadn't left my side since. I could feel her gratitude that I hadn't gotten myself killed. Though she clearly lacked faith in my ability to protect myself, I appreciated her concern.

I turned, wiping the sweat from my brow.

My friends sat in lawn chairs that Nix had conjured. They were a far cry from my parents' thrones, but those were just creepy. The room itself gleamed with a spic-and-span shine. Connor's hearth witch skills extended to magical cleaning, and it brightened my heart to see the place looking decent. He hadn't done the whole castle while I practiced—it was far too big—but at least this room looked good.

"You know, if I got rid of those thrones, we could put a bowling alley in here," I said, trying to lighten my mood.

Laughter echoed in the stone room, but it didn't make me feel much better.

Draka and I joined my friends, each taking a lawn chair.

"Thanks again for all your help, guys." I smiled at them.

Cass and Aidan held hands, Nix lounged with Pond Flower at her side, and Claire and Connor stopped their bickering to smile at me. Even Cade was here. But it was the pride in Roarke's grin that really made me frown. Why would he look at me like that? I'd failed. There was nothing to be proud of.

"You handled yourself well at the Shadows' castle," he said. "If you hadn't sent Pond Flower to us, we'd never have awoken."

"That was a genius plan on the Shadows' part," I said. "It's really the only way to keep you guys contained."

Nix cracked her knuckles in an exaggerated fashion. "It's true. We're very powerful."

All joking aside, they were powerful. But the Shadows were smart. Smart enough that they'd beaten us to the punch pretty much every time.

My heart sank at the reminder. "Aethelred's prediction came true. I did fail."

Nix nodded. "Yeah. But that was fate."

"Can't fight fate," Cass said.

I believed that. It was the reason that Aethelred's prophecy had sent me into a tailspin. I didn't want to be the Demise. I wanted to be the Guardian.

Clearly, I'd have to work for it.

"You didn't do exactly what the Shadows wanted you to do," Draka said. "If they'd had their way, the portal would be fully operational right now. Because you resisted their pull, the portal is much slower. Not even fully operational yet."

That was a small mercy, knowing that I'd mitigated the damage. "But demons are still flowing onto earth. Faster with every moment. And they don't need an

Earthbound sponsor. There's no limit to how many can come."

"We'll handle that," Roarke said. "We'll find the portal and shut it down. Then deal with the demons who've already escaped."

"However many there are," I said. It would be a challenge. Hundreds, maybe thousands, of demons.

"And we've already had some luck shutting down another portal," Nix said. "And that time, we didn't have you."

I smiled at the memory of the wayward portal from this summer. "That's a whole different matter. No demons were flooding the earth in that scenario."

Getting rid of them was my real concern. How fast were they flowing through now? And where to? It'd only been about six hours since we'd left the Underworld.

"True." Cass frowned. "But that's okay. We've got this."

"Especially now that we have that magical lump of lava thing," I said.

"Yeah, any idea what that is?" Cass asked.

"Not a clue," I said. "But hopefully it will come in handy. We're going to need all the help we can get."

"You'll have to find the location of the portal's exit," Cade said. "You can't return to the Shadows' stronghold."

The memory of the thousands of demons made me grimace. "Yeah, I know. We'll never win that battle. Not if we came at it from that angle. Problem is, I don't know which angle is the right one."

"We'll figure it out," Nix said.

"Yeah." Cass grinned. "We always do."

I groaned, though I was grateful to have my friends at my back. "Don't jinx us! Knock on your head."

Roarke squeezed my hand, then let go and knocked on his head.

I grinned at him. "At least someone has some sense around here."

And what we occasionally lacked in sense, we made up for in magical power. And loyalty. And hopefully, smarts. I could only hope it would be enough. Because what was coming for us was bigger than anything we'd ever faced before.

THANK YOU FOR READING!

I hope you enjoyed reading this book as much as I enjoyed writing it. Reviews are so helpful to authors. I really appreciate all reviews, both positive and negative. If you want to leave one, you can do so at Amazon or GoodReads.

AUTHOR'S NOTE

Thank you so much for reading *Magic Wild!* It was one of my favorite books to write, and I hope you enjoyed reading it as much as I enjoyed writing it. As with all of my books, I included historical and mythological elements. If you're interested in reading more about that, read on. At the end, I'll talk a bit about why Del and her *deirfiúr* are treasure hunters and how I try to make that fit with archaeology's ethics (which don't condone treasure hunting, as I'm sure you might have guessed). I spoke about this in the Author's Notes for the other books in the series, so if you've read any of those, then you've read this. But it's important stuff, so I wanted to include it here for anyone who missed it before.

Now, onto the history and mythology in *Magic Wild!* The first adventure in the book—into the swamps of Florida—was inspired by a recent trip to the Everglades. The river of grass is an amazing place, and home to the mythical Skunk Ape, which is Florida's version of Bigfoot, though he can also appear in North Carolina and Arkansas. He is so named for the odor he emits—it's supposed to be a bit like rotting cabbage, though I've never had the privilege of sniffing him for myself (thanks fates, since I lack Del's and Roarke's ability to get away from him). One of the most fascinating stories about the Skunk Ape is that sightings became so common in the 1970's that in 1977, Florida State Representative Paul Nuckolls attempted to pass a bill that would make it a misdemeanor to "take, possess, harm or molest anthropoid or humanoid animals." The bill never passed, but I can't help but admire the spirit of the attempt—and I think Del would too.

As for the town in the middle of the Everglades—there aren't any towns on stilts, but there are collections of houses that date back to the early 20th century. They're used primarily as fishing outposts today, but will soon return to the ownership of the state and a period of Florida's history will be gone for good. In fairness, the state is attempting to protect the wildlife of the Everglades, so good comes with the bad.

Machu Picchu is one of the places that epitomizes *Amazing Archaeological Site*, so it was high time I included it in a book. Though I don't say it directly in the text, the magical Incate settlement is based off of Machu Picchu, which was built by the Inca (see what I did there with the names?). The Inca built Machu Picchu around 1450 and abandoned it about one hundred years later when the Spanish arrived in Peru. Machu Picchu was never found by the Spanish, but it is theorized by some scholars that many of the inhabitants died from smallpox brought by the invaders.

Unfortunately, I haven't had the opportunity to visit Machu Picchu, but the internet is a great source for descriptions of the site. The current Machu Picchu has been partially restored, but when American Hiram Bingham first visited the site and brought it to the attention of the international community, it was much like how Del first discovered the Incate settlement—covered in vegetation with the buildings severely broken down. One of the most incredible features was the fountain that flowed down the mountainside.

As for the obsidian that the Incate healer coveted, samples were found at Machu Picchu, indicating long distance trade. Obsidian was used for weapons, tools, and ceremonial items by many cultures. When properly processed, obsidian can possess the sharpest edge in the world—sharper than any steel or metal—because the edge can be only three nanometers thick.

Zerzura, the city in the oasis, is based off of a mythical city that is said to be located in the deserts of Egypt or Libya. It appeared in texts as early as the 13th century and the buildings were supposed to be made of white stone. As with many lost cities, it is said to be full of treasure. Nineteenth and twentieth century explorers have searched for the city but never found it.

One last neat fact that I included in this book, and also in one of Cass's books, is that camels really can hold water bottles in their teeth and drink from them. Google has a lot of photos—check them out, they're really cool.

That's it for the historical influences in *Magic Wild*. However, one of the most important things about this book is how Del and her *deirfiúr* treat artifacts and their business, Ancient Magic. This is the part of the Author's Note that is written in the other books, so if you've read any of those, this'll be a repeat. But it's important enough that I like to include it in all my books. My conscience wouldn't rest otherwise.

As I'm sure you know, archaeology isn't quite like Indiana Jones (for which I'm both grateful and bitterly disappointed). Sure, it's exciting and full of travel. However, booby-traps are not as common as I expected. Total number of booby-traps I have encountered in my career: zero. Still hoping, though.

When I chose to write a series about archaeology and treasure hunting, I knew I had a careful line to tread. There is a big difference between these two activities. As much as I value artifacts, they are not treasure. Not even the gold artifacts. They are pieces of our history that contain valuable information, and as such, they belong to all of us. Every artifact that is excavated should be properly conserved and stored in a museum so that everyone can have access to our history. No one single person can own history, and I believe very strongly that individuals should not own artifacts. Treasure hunting is the pursuit of artifacts for personal gain.

So why did I make Del and her *deirfiúr* treasure hunters? I'd have loved to call them archaeologists, but nothing about Cass's work is like archaeology. Archaeology is a very laborious, painstaking process— and it certainly doesn't involve selling artifacts. That wouldn't work for the fast-paced, adventurous series that I had planned for *Dragon's Gift*. Not to mention the fact that dragons are famous for coveting treasure.

Considering where the *deirfiúr* got their skills from, it just made sense to call them treasure hunters.

Even though I write urban fantasy, I strive for accuracy. The *deirfiúr* don't engage in archaeological practices—therefore, I cannot call them archaeologists. I also have a duty as an archaeologist to properly represent my field and our goals—namely, to protect and share history. Treasure hunting doesn't do this. One of the biggest battles that archaeology faces today is protecting cultural heritage from thieves.

I debated long and hard about not only what to call the heroines of this series, but also about how they would do their jobs. I wanted it to involve all the cool things we think about when we think about archaeology—namely, the Indiana Jones stuff, whether it's real or not. But I didn't know quite how to do that while still staying within the bounds of my own ethics. I can cut myself and other writers some slack because this is fiction, but I couldn't go too far into smash and grab treasure hunting.

I consulted some of my archaeology colleagues to get their take, which was immensely helpful. Wayne Lusardi, the State Maritime Archaeologist for Michigan, and Douglas Inglis and Veronica Morris, both archaeologists for Interactive Heritage, were immensely helpful with ideas. My biggest problem was figuring out how to have the heroines steal artifacts from tombs and then sell them and still sleep at night. Everything I've just said is pretty counter to this, right?

That's where the magic comes in. The heroines aren't after the artifacts themselves (they put them back where they found them, if you recall)—they're after the magic that the artifacts contain. They're more like magic hunters than treasure hunters. That solved a big part of my problem. At least they were putting the artifacts back. Though that's not proper archaeology, I could let it pass. At least it's clear that they believe they shouldn't keep the artifact or harm the site. But the SuperNerd in me said, "Well, that magic is part of the artifact's context. It's important to the artifact and shouldn't be removed and sold."

Now *that* was a problem. I couldn't escape my SuperNerd self, so I was in a real conundrum. Fortunately, that's where the immensely intelligent Wayne Lusardi came in. He suggested that the magic could have an expiration date. If the magic wasn't used before it decayed, it could cause huge problems. Think explosions and tornado spells run amok. It could ruin the entire site, not to mention possibly cause injury and death. That would be very bad.

So now you see why Del and her *deirfiúr* don't just steal artifacts to sell them. Not only is selling the magic cooler, it's also better from an ethical standpoint, especially if the magic was going to cause problems in the long run. These aren't perfect solutions—the perfect solution would be sending in a team of archaeologists to carefully record the site and remove the dangerous magic—but that wouldn't be a very fun book.

Thanks again for reading (especially if you got this far!). I hope you enjoyed the story and will stick with Del on the rest of her adventure!

ACKNOWLEDGMENTS

Thank you, Ben, for everything. There would be no books without you.

Thank you to Jena O'Connor and Lindsey Loucks for your excellent editing. The book is immensely better because of you! And thank you to Rebecca Frank for the beautiful cover. You really bring Del to life. Thank you to Crystal Jeffs, for your help with continuity in the story. Your keen eye saved the day!

The Dragon's Gift series is a product of my two lives: one as an archaeologist and one as a novelist. Combining these two took a bit of work. I'd like to thank my friends, Wayne Lusardi, the State Maritime Archaeologist for Michigan, and Douglas Inglis and Veronica Morris, both archaeologists for Interactive Heritage, for their ideas about how to have a treasure hunter heroine that doesn't conflict too much with archaeology's ethics. The Author's Note contains a bit more about this if you are interested.

GLOSSARY

Alpha Council - There are two governments that enforce law for supernaturals—the Alpha Council and the Order of the Magica. The Alpha Council governs all shifters. They work cooperatively with the Alpha Council when necessary—for example, when capturing FireSouls.

Blood Sorceress - A type of Magica who can create magic using blood.

Conjurer - A Magica who uses magic to create something from nothing. They cannot create magic, but if there is magic around them, they can put that magic into their conjuration.

Dark Magic - The kind that is meant to harm. It's not necessarily bad, but it often is.

Deirfiúr - Sisters in Irish.

Demons - Often employed to do evil. They live in various hells but can be released upon the earth if you know how to get to them and then get them out. If they are killed on Earth, they are sent back to their hell.

Dragon Sense - A FireSoul's ability to find treasure. It is an internal sense that pulls them toward what they seek. It is easiest to find gold, but they can find anything or anyone that is valued by someone.

Elemental Mage – A rare type of mage who can manipulate all of the elements.

Enchanted Artifacts – Artifacts can be imbued with magic that lasts after the death of the person who put the magic into the artifact (unlike a spell that has not been put into an artifact—these spells disappear after the Magica's death). But magic is not stable. After a period of time—hundreds or thousands of years depending on the circumstance—the magic will degrade. Eventually, it can go bad and cause many problems.

Fire Mage – A mage who can control fire.

FireSoul - A very rare type of Magica who shares a piece of the dragon's soul. They can locate treasure and steal the gifts (powers) of other supernaturals. With practice, they can manipulate the gifts they steal, becoming the strongest of that gift. They are despised and feared. If they are caught, they are thrown in the Prison of Magical Deviants.

The Great Peace - The most powerful piece of magic ever created. It hides magic from the eyes of humans.

Hearth Witch – A Magica who is versed in magic relating to hearth and home. They are often good at potions and protective spells and are also very perceptive when on their own turf.

Magica - Any supernatural who has the power to create magic—witches, sorcerers, mages. All are governed by the Order of the Magica.

The Origin - The descendent of the original alpha shifter. They are the most powerful shifter and can turn into any species.

Order of the Magica - There are two governments that enforce law for supernaturals—the Alpha Council and the Order of the Magica. The Order of the Magica govern all Magica. They work cooperatively with the Alpha Council when necessary—for example, when capturing FireSouls.

Phantom - A type of supernatural that is similar to a ghost. They are incorporeal. They feed off the misery and pain of others, forcing them to relive their greatest nightmares and fears. They do not have a fully functioning mind like a human or supernatural. Rather, they are a shadow of their former selves. Half-bloods are extraordinarily rare.

Seeker - A type of supernatural who can find things. FireSouls often pass off their dragon sense as Seeker power.

Shifter - A supernatural who can turn into an animal. All are governed by the Alpha Council.

Transporter - A type of supernatural who can travel anywhere. Their power is limited and must regenerate after each use.

Warden of the Underworld - A one of a kind position created by Roarke. He keeps order in the Underworld.

ABOUT LINSEY

Before becoming a writer, Linsey Hall was a nautical archaeologist who studied shipwrecks from Hawaii and the Yukon to the UK and the Mediterranean. She credits fantasy and historical romances with her love of history and her career as an archaeologist. After a decade of tromping around the globe in search of old bits of stuff that people left lying about, she settled down and started penning her own romance novels. Her Dragon's Gift series draws upon her love of history and the paranormal elements that she can't help but include.

Linsey@LinseyHall.com
www.LinseyHall.com
https://twitter.com/HiLinseyHall
https://www.facebook.com/LinseyHallAuthor

BONNIE
DOON
PRESS

ISBN 978-1-942085-36-2